JUST ONE MO

JUST ONE MO

By Mark T. Sneed

DEDICATION

To my mother, family and friends who continue to inspire, encourage and challenge me to be a better person, even when they are not around.

THANK YOU

To all the unsung dreamers, visionaries, believers, questioners, who possess the faith and belief in their convictions despite what others try to say or attempt to shout down what is impossible. Thank you for attempting to prove your beliefs, dreams and ideas not to spite but to enlighten others of what a different perspective and trust can manifest in the scope of what is possible.

JUST ONE MO

JUST ONE MO
By Mark T. Sneed

Prologue.

It was 2020 when I began at Gee Dub, George Washington Carver High School, a predominately black high school in the heart of Oakland, in the San Francisco Bay Area of Northern California. As a freshman I was determined to get into the best colleges, but I knew I was going to need some help to make that happen.

One day while I was hiding in my counselor's office, I happened upon one of those college magazines which gave me the idea of how to make my college plans a reality. The cover had a girl on it who was dark skinned and had big eyes and looked a little like my cousin Robin. Valerie Cooper, the girl on the cover, grinned from her college dorm. She was from Atlanta. The article was about how this girl amassed nearly one hundred thousand dollars in scholarships for her college education. The girl had begun her scholarship hunt during her sophomore year and by the beginning of her senior year she had scraped together, just by applying for scholarships, sixty thousand dollars in scholarship money. By the time she walked the stage at her high school graduation Valerie Cooper had over one hundred thousand dollars in scholarships for college.

In the magazine with Cooper was this short article on community service and colleges looking for unique and passionate students.

"Every college wants the best and the brightest, but they know the best and the brightest are not just found in the classroom. The college admission teams are in the business of looking into the future and forecasting what might be. These college admission teams are fortune tellers. They have in recent years found the best and brightest that shock the world are not always students with 4.0 GPA or with perfect SAT or ACT scores. The students with the greatest potential are the ones that concentrate on bettering their community. The student that is passionate about some issue, any issue is the student that distinguishes him or herself more than the 4.0 GPA."

Those words, not unlike the Valerie Cooper article, stuck with me. So, I had goals as my sophomore year at Gee Dub came to an end.

I read Valerie Cooper's article when I was a sophomore at Gee Dub. I decided I was going to apply for no less than fifty scholarships and get accepted to every college I applied to because I had a plan.

I took the magazine with Valerie Cooper and the community service article with me. I slipped the magazine in my backpack. I figured anytime I was unsure or uncertain I could unzip my backpack and look at one of the two articles for inspiration.

Now, I have to admit I was cocky and smug by my senior year at Gee Dub. Based on the raw footage Cue had shown us there was just no way any school would deny any of our entry. In one summer, I had guaranteed the entries of over a dozen students into any of the prestigious college or university in the nation and become an Internet sensation. All the events had seemed random and scattered at times, but they all seemed essential for my plan and altruistic feat the end of my Junior summer and the year I became a senior at George Washington Carver High School.

Of course, on the other side of all the good I had nearly been thrown in jail, as had the dozen others involved, but the threat of jail became meaningless as soon as Cue, Derricka and Tanza uploaded a series of videos. Everyone in our ragtag group went from small potatoes to instant importance.

Our bending of the laws faded compared to the reuniting of a misguided wanderer with his own. It was, as I thought about it, poetic in a way.

Once back in the states we were asked by many news sources for interviews. I was interviewed by the biggest newspapers. Half a dozen times I was on national television.

The year before I became a senior at Gee Dub, I wasn't sure I would be accepted into any college, let alone every college I was planning on applying to that year. I had made a mess of things the end of my freshmen year. I had tried to best Icarus and flown too close to the sun and come crashing down, alone, battered and a pariah. The results of that foul up endangered all my plans at Gee Dub and beyond, but all that comes later.

Table of Content

Chapter 1.

Let me begin at the beginning of my four-year adventure. My first year at Gee Dub I was so excited. After I graduated from Frederick Douglass Junior High School all I could think about was being a student at Gee Dub.

Now, there were some simple complications on going to Gee Dub. I lived on MacArthur Boulevard and Gee Dub was in the middle of Knolls hills. If I took the bus, I did my research, I would have to take two buses to get to school. Based on my research, a bus ride would take me anywhere from ninety to two hours, one way.

Thankfully, my mother arranged through my aunt Arna, for my cousin BB to pick me up and drive me to school my freshman year at Gee Dub. BB was a star at Gee Dub. BB and I were friendly, but he was three years my senior and at times a bit of a bonehead. While I was at Frederick Douglass, I helped BB with some of his math homework. He was this larger-than-life character who I was related to and I tried to keep the fanboy thing to a minimum. To make BB know I not seeing him as a paycheck or rising star or whatever I pretended not to care too much about my cousin's fabulous life. We had a strange and friendly relation where he and I never gave each other a break. I liked giving him a hard time every time I could. It was our thing.

When I climbed into his Mustang the first day of school a little after seven o'clock in the morning BB had this smirk on his face.

"What?"

"You okay?"

"Yeah," I smirked.

"You look a little weirder than usual," BB smiled.

"I'm good," I said, a little nervously. It was the first day of high school. Things were going to be entirely different. I had graduated from junior high one of the smartest and wanted to prove myself. Unlike BB I was not gifted physically. I was just this skin and bones kid with big eyes and high cheekbones, I inherited from my mom. My head was big, compared to my body. I had no muscles to mention. I was not athletic by any stretch of the imagination.

I was sure BB was looking at me the first day dressed in my large collared white shirt and baggy ironed khaki trousers with my black North Face backpack on my lap, in his car and thinking to ask his dad if I was really related to him. I looked at the tall and muscular BB under the steering wheel. He was dressed in the same thing as me, but on him it looked like it was tailor made. He was six-foot-four-inches of athletic strength. BB was coffee brown and always dressed nicely. His hair was always neatly cut and his fade was never lacking.

He looked at me with those dark brown eyes and I could see he wanted to say something but held back. I thought about the pause and thought I knew what BB was thinking but refused to test my theory. People did not like to feel I could read them. I learned that lesson the hard way. As BB pulled away from the curb and we headed to school to start the school year I just remained quiet.

BB liked hip hop and rap and anytime I climbed into the Mustang he was playing one or the other. That morning we were listening to a rapper I heard a thousand times and could not name. He was rapping about looking through the peephole. The rapper's delivery was hypnotic. I found myself listening to the beat and felt my head bopping.

"You okay, brainiac," BB asked as I settled in. I nodded.

I loved to ride in his blue 2013 Mustang. It was his cherished possession. He loved his car and was always fussing with it. He drove the pony like he was either cruising or late for something. There was no in between for BB. That morning he drove as if he was cruising.

We rolled past the freeway entrance and I looked at BB and then back out the window.

"So, moms tells me you nearly died over the summer," BB smiled.

"Nearly," I repeated, pinching my lips nervously.

"What happened," he said.

I shook my head.

"Spill," BB said as he drove. I paused. Our relationship was built on honesty. If I did something embarrassing, then I had to tell. The same rules applied to BB.

"Well, over the summer I was trying to see a meteor that was passing by and knew I couldn't get to the planetarium. So, I came up with a plan. I thought I had things figured out and it was dark, and I did something stupid," I explained looking out of the window.

"Yeah, that's obvious," BB said with a smile.

I looked out the window and saw the younger kids walking on the streets early in the morning. It was late August and in a couple of days we would have Labor Day off. I wanted to change the topic.

"Spill."

I took a deep breath. "Well, you know that cellphone tower on School Avenue? Well, there was this meteor shower and I wanted to see it. I had been thinking about astronomy. So, I wanted to see if I was really interested or just sort of interested."

"Come on," BB said with a big grin on his magically transformed clown-like face.

"You know I don't really like heights much, but I decided to just climb up the tower. In my mind it seemed to make sense. All I had to do was climb and not look down." I paused.

"I'm loving this," BB said, his wide smile broadening across his chestnut-colored face. His smile spread with the details of my climbing on the cellphone tower and getting stuck three hundred feet in the air.

"Wait, how did you get past the gate?"

"I'm nearly three hundred feet in the air and about to fall and all you focus on is me outsmarting a gate?"

"No," BB said, sheepishly. "No," He paused. "I was just.... Go on."

"Well, someone must have seen me get past the gate and climb on the tower and called the police or the fire department. Thank God they did. I don't know how long I could have stayed up there without falling to my death."

"Stuck up on a tower like a cat in a tree," BB smiled. He shook his head and chuckled. BB let a smile crease his brown face. Under his thick eyebrows he cut his dark eyes in my direction. "Why you do something like that Auggie?"

"I thought it made sense. The higher I could get the better the chance to see the meteor shower."

There was a pause. I filled the silence with more words.

"I couldn't see the meteor shower from our house. I thought about climbing on the roof but there's all those apartment buildings near us blocking the skyline. Needed to be above the apartments to get a good look."

"My mom and your moms think you were trying to do something...stupid," BB said with a more serious look.

"What?" I said, suddenly insulted. "You know me. I'm not stupid. I just made a miscalculation," I said.

"A miscalculation," BB repeated. He was driving and not really looking at me. It sounded like he was reading the news.

"Yeah, a mistake. I thought I could get a better vantage point on the cell tower and just made a mistake," I admitted. I thought about the police car which showed up first and then the cell phone company van. There were easily a dozen people standing around the tower that night of the meteor shower. By the time the fire engine arrived there was a small crowd gathered.

"How come you didn't climb down," BB asked.

"I couldn't," I said, shaking my head.

I could not make myself come down off the tower. Heights were my kryptonite. The fire department sent a fireman in on a hook and ladder to rescue me from the cellphone tower. The fireman was a big, strong man dressed like he was going to a fire. He reached out and plucked me off the tower like I was a scared kitten.

"Relax, kid," the fireman said, once I was in the safety of the bucket. The fireman and I descended and knew I had to face a lot of questions.

The police had to interview me. The fire department filled out some papers. Then the city crisis manager, Mister Rowan, showed up. He was this thin faced white man who smelled of cigarettes and alcohol. He was dressed in a wrinkled brown suit. Rowan looked like he had just woken up or never gone to sleep the night before. He had a five o'clock shadow even though it was nearly ten o'clock at night.

Rowan interviewed me right there at the cell tower with about fifty people watching. It was quick and every question was to be expected.

You trying to harm yourself? Had you planned this out beforehand? Do you feel trapped? Depressed? Did you intend to harm yourself or others?

My mom showed up. I was sort of surprised by the time I set foot back on earth she wasn't there. She showed up about five or ten minutes later.

Mister Rowan gave my mom his card. "I don't think he intended to harm himself," he said a little louder than my mother preferred. "Watch him." He handed her a pamphlet. "If he exhibits any symptoms call. There's no harm in being careful."

"So, you weren't trying to kill yourself," BB said, with a serious look.

"What? No," I said.

"Okay, cool," BB said snapping me out of my summer memories. "Mom told me to check on you. To make sure you weren't thinking about offing yourself or anything."

I shook those summer thoughts from my head. "Why would I want to kill myself? I am a freshman this year. I get to lay the groundwork for my high school career. By the time I'm a senior everyone will be talking about me at Gee Dub."

I had all these grand plans. I was going to participate in all the academic afterschool activities. I had sketched it out, generally. I wanted to join the debate team. I also wanted to join the chess club. I was good at debate. I was pretty sure I could beat most people in chess. I had talent.

"Just think in ten months I will have eight times to get on the honor roll and be a sophomore and prepare for college," I said to BB, who only shook his head as he drove toward Gee Dub.

We turned onto Dempsey Street and crossed the train tracks and climbed a short slight rise and to the left were dozens of homes which had been there forever. To the right sat the acres of land which held George Washington Carver High School.

BB turned the Mustang to the left and the first thing I saw was the chain-link fencing around the football field. There were bleachers where students and parents would sit during a game. There was a scoreboard which sat dark but held the GWCHS Knights emblem and the words Visitor. The field sat in front of the main building.

The Mustang turned right and slowly entered the parking lot. I had a great view of the chain-link fence which ran the entire length of the rear of the school and separated the dozen or so wooden fences of houses which rested on the other side of the school fence. In the parking lot there were thirty or forty cars already parked closest to the exit.

BB did not speed up or slow down but let the Mustang pull itself forward barely touching the gas. There were a group of boys wearing letterman jackets gathered around the cars closest to the exit. BB lowered himself just a little more in his seat as his Mustang inched past the boys wearing the letterman jackets.

"What up BB," one of the dorks said. BB nodded and he and I slid through the high school parking lot.

"Baseball dorks," BB said out of the corner of his mouth as the Mustang slinked toward the rear of the parking lot. I nodded seeing the boys looking at me and realizing they were looking at BB.

I sat and tried to remember all the information BB had given me about Gee Dub. I had come to the school often during the winter to see my cousin play basketball. He sometimes would walk me around the campus. I felt I had a pretty good understanding of the layout of the school, thanks to BB.

There was a lot of activity the first day of school. There were easily two dozen cars lined up dropping off students. There was a yellow bus inching its way toward the exit of the teardrop parking lot. The Mustang moved away from the main entrance and the knots of students, parents and cars all at the front of the school and toward the rear of the school and the tennis courts. I craned my neck to see all the faces of students I did not know.

Not knowing students made me excited and nervous all at the same time. BB didn't seem to care about my nervousness. He slowed.

Parked near the rear gate of the fence which led to the tennis courts were a dozen cars of another group of sports stars of Gee Dub. BB parked next to a Honda Ridgeline. I climbed out of the Mustang. BB stalled. He climbed out reluctantly and leaned on his car and looked back toward the front of the school. He seemed in no hurry to start the school year.

"You okay, BB," I asked.

"Yeah," BB said, and I wasn't convinced.

"What's the problem, big boy, you worried about finishing strong?"

BB smirked. I smiled. I hit a soft spot. I could have let it go.

"You know this year is really meaningless if you think about it. I mean, as long as you don't screw up. The colleges already have a gauge on you. The recruits coming this year are late to the party. They may show up, but they're coming just to be sure. All they want now is for you to maintain your grades and not fall off," I smiled.

"You know that you can be a pain, right?"

"Why," I giggled. "You being a rising star and all, and college wants you. So, just don't crack this year. Don't break under the pressure. You'll be fine," I smiled.

BB rolled his eyes and shook his head, silently watching me.

"Besides, that's why you love me," I said.

"I don't love you, Auggie," BB said with a shake of his head.

"We blood. You got to love me. That's the rules," I said and felt my smile pull up the right corner of my lips.

"Alright," BB said, shaking his head.

"Hey, BB, if you need help," I said from the side of the Mustang. "I will help you. I have to start thinking about my senior year too."

He nodded. BB smiled. "Moms made me promise to take you to school," BB said, raising his gigantic paw. "I'll give you a ride home if you are at the car before I leave. If you ain't, you aint. This week I won't be too hard on you. But I'm out usually at three fifty, after all the traffic dies down a bit." He paused and added, "As soon as basketball practice starts though, you will have to figure out another way to get home. Unless you willing to wait."

Waiting? Figuring it out meant getting a ride back to my home, just thirty minutes north by car. If, God forbid, I walked home from school it would take me... honestly, I had never imagined walking home from school. We had driven for twenty-five or thirty minutes and I hadn't paid attention to any street signs. The first thing on my list was to figure out alternative ways home.

I smiled despite my concern for another way home. It was August. Basketball practice didn't start for at least three months. I had time to figure things out. I could always sit around and wait.

I walked away from BB with my slight grin fading. I walked to the double red doors and paused. I spun around and looked at my six-foot-four-inch-tall cousin wearing khaki trousers, new white basketball sneakers, a collared white polo shirt and a gray zip front lightweight jacket that morning.

I checked my wristwatch. It was not eight o'clock. School was over at three thirty. Seven and a half hours of learning every day.

I knew BB was going to leave school as soon as three fifty ticked off, when it wasn't basketball season. So, I had to be in the parking lot or coming out of this very door no later than three forty-five or he might be wheeling out of the parking lot.

Chapter 2.

Eighth month of the year

I thought all that as I opened one of the red doors which signaled the exterior entrance to the fifteen hundred student campus. As I entered, I smiled at the red and gray lockers and the continual red and gray tile pattern on the floors which pointed toward the end of the hallway.

The rear of the building held a dozen classrooms on the exterior wall. Each door was closed. On a tile next to the door was the room number and beneath it the name of each teacher. There was a foot wide six-foot-high by two-foot-wide window in each door. I stopped and looked inside one of the darkened rooms. There were thirty desks. On the far side of the classroom was a teacher's desk.

I walked past the half dozen classrooms and was greeted by a long hallway which ran the entire length of Gee Dub. It had to be two football fields long. There were knots of students dressed in gray shirts and khaki trousers up and down the hall. The girls were required to wear white blouses and gray skirts or pants. I brushed my polo shirt and tried to ignore the few faces I recognized from junior high and the eyes watching me moving to the front of school.

Near the basketball gym, where I had sat and watched BB play hundreds of times, I saw Jesse, Del and Percy and a few faces I didn't know sneering at me as I approached. Jesse didn't like me since the fourth grade for some unknown reason.

"Hey, psycho coming," Jesse called as I approached.

"Heard you tried to off yourself this summer," Del sneered. I looked at Del.

Del was a pretty boy trying to be a tough and like Jesse didn't like me. He had a legitimate reason I suppose. I had complained when I saw him smacking a girl's butt to make her cry.

Del got in trouble. He never forgot me retelling what he had done after he denied it. His parents were called as a result of his lying.

The third member of my personal hate group was Percy Carter. Percy Carter was a whip thin kid with big eyes and a crooked smile. He was the class clown. Wearing a Boss Baby backpack and glass frames without lenses he grinned at Del's comment. Like every boy at Gee Dub he wore khaki pants, white collared shirt and around his neck hung the new gray and red trimmed Gee Dub ID badge.

I stopped. I knew I shouldn't have stopped. I should have just let what Del said pass, but I didn't. I shook my head. I turned and squared off against Del and spoke.

"Butt munch, I did not try to end myself any more than your fat ass mama tried to get pregnant and have you," I said, staring at Del ready to fight.

There was an explosion of laughter and elbowing by the dozen kids standing around as Del froze. Some looked around like Del had disappeared. Some jumped up and down. Del just stood there. I kept walking.

"Damn, Del, say something," someone said with a laugh.

"Oh, yeah," was all I heard as I continued walking up the hallway. My mom told me time and time again never start fights, but make sure you ended them. I looked back and people were shaking their heads and pushing on Del's chest like he needed to be resuscitated.

I turned and focused on the front of school. I passed through a knot of students and arrived at the front of the high school. Students were taking pictures, getting ID badges and their class schedules as well as just milling around talking about their summer vacations. Parents, teachers and the principal were all in the same area.

BB told me every year, in the first week, Gee Dub was like trying to get backstage at a concert. The first five days of school saw the biggest group of people trying to register, get class schedules and their papers filled out. Thanks to BB all my papers had been turned in early by my cousin over the summer. I scanned the tables and found the one with a paper tent sign labeled: Pre-Reg. I walked to the quiet table where a banana hued girl with long wavy black hair sat reading a book.

"Hi, I'm August Manning, I need my class schedule," I said. The girl, a yellow-skinned beauty with big brown and green eyes, hoop earrings and the most bored look on her face looked up from her book. The girl looked at me for a long moment before she stopped reading. She dog eared the page she was on and sat the book on the table and smiled, bored.

"August Manning," she repeated and leafed through the small stack of papers in front of her. She pulled out my schedule and looked at me, curiously. The girl studied my paper schedule for half a second and twisted her lips as if she wanted to say something. She smiled instead and nodded. "Here you go," the nameless girl said, handing me my schedule.

"Why didn't they preregister?" I said looking at the crowd.

"You got me," the girl said and returned to reading her book. "Don't forget to get your ID," the girl said pointing to the left.

"Thanks," I said as I walked away. I scanned the crowded front of the school. I weaved my way through the crowd of parents, students and adults dressed for the first day of school. In the entryway to another hallway at the top of the front of school stood the ID photo area.

From what I could see of the ID photo area the set-up was basic. A blue backdrop. A stool. Tape on the ground. And the photographer.

I got in line behind three other people and waited. Occasionally, I looked back and into the sea of faces registering and trying to get their first day at school started. Ahead of me were a boy and two girls. I didn't know them and just stood waiting silently. The boy, in front of me, looked back and we locked eyes. He was a round faced kid the color of toast wearing a simple dark blue backpack. He had apple cheeks and a dull look on his round face.

"I'm Fred," the apple cheeked boy said and lifted a balled-up fist.

"Auggie," I said and lifted my balled fist and exchanged a dap.

"Where did you go to school last year," Fred asked.

I didn't answer. Instead, I lifted my chin in the direction of the photographer. The girl was posing. The photographer took her picture.

Fred turned and took a step forward and then turned back. "I went to Parkside," Fred said with pride. I knew of Parkside. It was a good school. It was one of the schools that continued to surprise academically and athletically.

"Didn't Dime Dame go to Parkside?"

Fred smiled broadly.

"Next," the photographer said.

"That's my cousin," Fred said stepping forward and being directed, by the photographer, to sit on the stool and look toward the plush Gee Dub knight dangling from a string to give all the students the look of star gazers.

Fred took his picture and instead of moving off, he waited. I sat and took my ID picture. I tried not to think about Fred, but his waiting did not allow me that luxury.

After I took my picture I climbed off the stool and there was Fred, smiling as he had before.

"Your ID should be ready in ten minutes. If you don't pick it up it will be given to you in your Advisory this week," the photographer said. I nodded. I was going to ask how the haters had their IDs, but I didn't care enough to bring it up or wait for an excuse.

"Well, you got any classes with me?"

Before I could answer a fashionable man, who had too much cologne on, walked up to me and smiled. He was dressed in a checkered vest, a red bow tie, a periwinkle blue collared shirt and camel brown trousers and matching leather shoes. The man was the color of fine sandpaper. He smiled and introduced himself.

"I'm Mister Davenport," he said and shook my hand. I adjusted my backpack and smiled or sort of grimaced. "You are August Manning?"

I nodded.

Fred looked confused. I looked from Mister Davenport to Fred and back.

"Young man," Mister Davenport said to Fred.

"Fred Martin, sir," Fred said.

"Well, will you excuse us Fred Martin, I have some things to discuss with August."

Fred nodded and reluctantly walked away. I smiled at Fred's lost dog look when he walked away and into the sea of faces in the front of school.

"I'm the school psychologist," Davenport said and as those words fell out of his mouth, I knew the next two or three minutes were all meant to make me comfortable. I listened and waited for the punchline. So, I listened to the man who smelled like flowers and a hint of wood.

"We have reached out to your mom already. We just need to make sure if you feel overwhelmed you have someone to talk to. So, for the first semester, as a precaution and more to make sure that your transition to high school is a success, you and I will meet once a week."

I didn't mind. It was not like I had a choice. I understood the situation. Gee Dub had to make sure I was mentally stable.

I nodded. I picked up my schedule and my ID badge and looked for my friends.

With all that happening my first year at Gee Dub was a thousand times better because I had good friends. Everyone, in our then little nameless group, had known each other since grade school. We weren't always on the best behaviors or in the nicest of relations, but everyone got along with one another. I suppose we all had our strengths and weaknesses.

Chapter 3.

Friends

There were five of us. No one was more important than the other, but together we were sort of special.

Me, I was smart and always trying to think ahead. For a long time, I wanted to be a scientist. I just loved the idea of discovering something or creating something. I had studied the stars. Now, I wanted to study robotics. I got good grades, but sometimes I struggled. Nothing came easy. Occasionally, I would fly off the handle and get into fights. It didn't happen often, but it happened. On the other side I was, at times, too sensitive and moody. I knew I had some things to work on.

Unlike me, Will was always cracking jokes or talking about movies and basketball or running the dozens. He was nearly five foot seven inches tall in eighth grade. Will imagined himself a basketball player, but he had small shoulders, short arms and a bit of a belly. He was incredibly smart in grade school and had this crazy brain which absorbed things and retained things most forgot. But he never used the knowledge to better his situation for some reason. He seemed distracted as we graduated junior high. He was my oldest friend and the one who gave me the most grief. Will was this weird kid I knew most of my life and didn't know at all.

Rome was the friend who wanted to be famous. He loved to sing. When he wasn't trying to crush people's dreams he sang. Rome always had his hair cut, trimmed and lined. He dressed up all the time. I think he expected to be discovered by a talent scout one day and dressed the part. When we wore T-shirts, cut-off jeans and sneakers he was wearing polo shirts, Bermuda shorts and Sperry Top Siders. He was trying desperately to be seen and noticed every day and in our neighborhood that desire made him a target. Some looked at him as a pretty boy or soft boy.

Of all of us, Rome, had money. His father was some famous music producer. We all knew his father was famous and he was always working with celebrities. Rome didn't tell anyone about his money.

"You know that my dad told me once that money is freedom and a prison at the same time," he said once in junior high.

"How?"

"Don't know," he smiled a toothy grin. "I guess that it is good in some ways, but on the other side you can't trust a lot of people because of it."

"Naw, man, that's stupid," Will explained. "Rich people don't know how to live with all that money. They be afraid someone is coming to steal it. So, they lock it up. That don't make no sense."

"It's a problem we ain't got to worry about," I laughed.

"Everyone wants better," Lew said.

"What you want?"

"Me? I don't know. I would love to make enough money so that my mom didn't have to work unless she wanted to," I said.

"Me, I want a Ra-Ra-Rolls Royce, a yacht, a man-man-mansion," Dre stammered. He took a deep breath. "All the stuff that Porky Pig got."

"You mean, Elmer Fudd," I corrected, with a smile.

Dre was the quiet and brooding one of our group. He was incredibly smart and loved numbers and all the aspects of math for some reason. Dre was a genius with numbers, but he had a bit of a speech impediment. Yet, in his math classes he was the one kid everyone went to for help.

Whatever the teacher threw at Dre in Math he took and spit back. After the first marking period Dre was the only person in our group to be moved to a higher math class. He did all right in his other classes but was average to incompetent with the required soft electives. He just didn't apply himself to them.

Dre struggled in the easiest of classes. He seemed completely confused on the purpose of Art class or foreign languages.

"I just don't un-un-understand why we need to paint things," Dre stuttered. "I-I-I mean we-we-we can buy art if-if-if we want art. If I go somewhere and-and-and don't know the lan-lan-language I'll hire a translator."

Dre had these grand goals. He wanted to start his own company. He was going to start a black software company which concentrated on gaming. He always seemed to be wrestling with some earth-shattering news. I always chalked it up to the fact he was the gray baby of the group. He was this tall, sand colored boy with wavy black hair and a square chin. Dre was nearly six-foot-tall and one-hundred-seventy-pounds when we graduated from junior high school. We all learned he had a white mother and his dad had disappeared long ago. That reality haunted him. It was the only thing to sink his spirit on a good day for some reason.

Lastly, there was Lew Benson, Mister Hug-A-Tree. He was our group conscious. He cared about so much. He loved the earth. He loved animals. He was an earth loving black kid. I think Lew was the first person to explain why we needed to recycle.

He did not just talk recycling he lived it. Somehow, he bought clothes which were new and made of recycled materials. The idea seemed impossible. New clothes made from used materials.

"When I grow up, I think I want to do something with ecology and law," Lew said.

Beyond his big ears, big eyes Lew was a bright yellow banana colored brother with a dimple in his chin. Will called it Lew's dimple his visible booty. Lew and Will were always at each other. They were friends but Will was always looking for an opening to prove his superiority.

All my plans nearly were derailed because of my first year at Gee Dub.

Now, I know it is a kind of cliché to say high school is a true measure of student's potential, but it is. In high school students are left to their own devices. Read somewhere the most racist, sexist, misogynistic, homophobic, xenophobic place in the nation is the high school system. Hate groups target high school students. Racists become extreme racists in high school.

It is also the place where students blossom and begin to become independent thinkers. High school students become future leaders. Students see the world differently in high school. At least, it was the way I saw it when I arrived in high school.

Gee Dub had the best athletic program in the East Bay. We were a powerhouse in all our sports. Every year Gee Dub sent a handful of athletes to state and local colleges. It was the rare few who were accepted to national colleges and universities.

Our principal, Mister Roger Allen, had high expectations. He had been at Gee Dub for nearly a decade. He did not tolerate anyone trying to skate through Gee Dub. He walked through the hallways checking on the nearly fifteen hundred students.

The teachers at Gee Dub were all top notch. The ones I ran into were strict and disciplined and had high expectations for us. Perhaps, that was one of the reasons I liked being a student at Gee Dub.

Academically, students at Gee Dub competed in debate, chess and oratorical contests each year. The Gee Dub debate team had won several debate tournaments. The chess team was competitive. Each year, thanks to the strong debate coaches, Gee Dub won or came in top five for the oratorical contests.

Socially, there was a diverse population. There were a bunch of black students at Gee Dub. There were 16% Hispanic in the halls and classrooms. In the freshman class there were Ricardo Alvarez, Felipe Luna and Martin Perez. 5% White. 4% other. At least, the data suggested the diversity. I never really noticed or paid that much attention.

Outstanding students went to the bigger colleges or universities. Some got full scholarships. Others got partial scholarships. As I walked through the main halls of Gee Dub, I often found myself looking at the big display case near the counseling office. The display was two display panels which featured all the students who graduated. It was an impressive list of 137 students out of 189 who were seniors before graduation from the year before. Next to that display was a distinctive list of athletic and academic scholarships awarded. Of the 137 nearly all were awarded at least one scholarship.

My first year I learned about the Gee Dub scholar, a distinguished honor at GWCHS. Usually, honors were reserved for athletes, but not at Gee Dub. Gee Dub scholars were respected and given lapel pins to wear and certificates, sometimes the scholars were asked to student teach in many classes where they excelled. Gee Dub scholars were peer tutors. They were distinguished by the same senior Gee Dub blazer and often asked by the athletic department to tutor academically challenged athletes. At Gee Dub, the athletes relied on Gee Dub scholars. With the Gee Dub scholar lapel pin (given after two consecutive honor roll placements) students were scholastic celebrities.

I had begun my freshman year at Gee Dub with my four friends from junior high school when things were simpler. In grade school and the first part of junior high all my friends were in the same classes. Now we were only in one class together, PE. During PE we talked and learned things about our bodies. It was one class I looked forward to because all my friends from junior high were there.

Before school and at lunch the five of us all gathered in the lunchroom and sat at our freshman table. There were two senior lunch tables closest to the steam tables. Most seniors did not eat in the cafeteria. There were four junior lunch tables, next to the senior tables. Some of the juniors, like the seniors chose not to eat in the cafeteria. Seniors and juniors were the only ones allowed to leave campus and get lunch. Behind the junior tables were six sophomore lunch tables. For freshman there were six lunch tables which sat at the rear of the lunchroom. Our table, the nerdy table, sat closest to the lunchroom exit.

At that table, with twenty other students, we talked about everything under the sun. At our lunch table we discussed math, science, history and all manner of things. Those walking by might overhear us arguing about artificial intelligence or which superhero was better Batman or Ironman. I leaned toward Batman. We discussed vampires, werewolves and zombies. There was nothing off limits at our end of the lunchroom table.

"You know we need a group name," Rome decided.

"What are you talking about?"

"All the best friends in high school have a group name," Rome continued. "I think we should be the New Five Heartbeats because of...me." Rome smiled. "You know, I am the singer."

"What you-you-you think, Will," Dre stammered.

"What? I'm focused on my academics," Will said with a frown. He had his History book in front of him.

"New Kids on the Block?"

"Think in your head," Will said.

"No one is worrying about a name," Lew concluded. He pointed to a table with a dozen girls sitting and laughing and talking.

High school was so different. It was bigger. It was faster. There was so much happening every day. I often imagined if I just went through one day focused on one thing, I would miss out on everything all around me at Gee Dub.

Eighteen weeks made up the first semester. I was scheduled to meet with Mister Davenport once a week that first semester. Once a week I met with the neatly dressed man the color of cashews. He was a handsome man who bordered on pretty and he knew it. Davenport creeped me out, just a little, because he looked like Rome might turned up one hundred.

The first time I officially met my psychologist he was sitting behind his desk in a room just off the library. It looked like the room was a converted closet. There was a desk near the entrance of the room with one of those floor lamps that looks like a hanging spider, a wooden conference table, which sat eight and another desk at the far end of the rectangular room. Like the other desk there was a floor lamp that was a silver version of the other spider lamp. There was no personal furniture, except the two standing lamps.

At the far desk I sat in a comfortable chair. I noticed Davenport had a bouncy ball to sit on as well, but it had been hidden by the conference table.

"So, August, how are you today?" Davenport smiled and seemed genuinely concerned. He listened. I didn't have much to say. I wasn't reluctant or stubborn, but I knew Davenport was listening for key words as he tried to ease into the real issue. I smiled as I spoke. Happy people didn't contemplate scary thoughts.

For thirty minutes Davenport poked and prodded me with his questions about my mental health.

"Do you feel isolated?"

"No," I said.

"Well, if you have any concerns you can talk to me. I'm here for you," the man dressed in an outfit ripped right out of GQ magazine said. I believed him. Thankfully, I had no concerns.

Usually, I would have just enough time to get back to PE to check in with Mister Smith, my PE teacher before class dismissed. It was only once a week. No big deal.

Maybe a couple of weeks after the first six weeks I made honor roll and Lew brought up the topic we all were curious about since our arrival at Gee Dub.

"Everyone wants a girlfriend in high school," Lew said with an eye roll at the end of the lunch table. "It's a big deal, in high school."

"Says who," said Rome with a shake of his head.

"The problem with girlfriends is-is-is the cra-cra-craziness of deal-deal-dealing with them," Dre managed.

"The problem with girlfriends is that for all the good parts the bad parts usually get you in trouble with everyone else," Rome said.

Dre nodded.

"Yeah, girls are cool and all, from afar," Will said with a smile.

Dre quickly added, "Like tigers."

"Right," I agreed.

"They are cool to look at, from a distance, but super dangerous up close."

"They'll rip you apart," Will joked.

Dre nodded. I looked around the table and saw everyone agreeing.

"Think it's for the best to avoid them for now," Rome said.

"Like the plague," I said with a laugh.

"At least until we-we-we figure things out," Dre said at the lunch table.

"I mean, I'm not saying that if Jennifer, over there, came and wanted to go to the movies with me I would turn her down," Lew countered.

We all looked in the direction Lew was looking and saw the second table filled with girls eating lunch and talking. Jennifer was one of twenty or so girls sitting at the table. Everyone, including me, looked at the table of girls.

"We need to be friendly," I said. "But at the same time be aware that our first priority here is learning."

"Yeah," Dre said.

"Remember every six weeks we have grades coming out," Rome said, turning back from the girl's table. "We have to focus."

"The next grades are in-in-in two weeks," Dre said.

Will pouted. Last marking period he had missed the honor roll with two bad grades. He was horrible in Science and English. Of the five of us, three had made the honor roll the first marking period. Lew, Dre and I had distinguished ourselves, academically.

"We all need to focus on books and sports or anything else but girls for at least the first year," Lew said.

"There's so much more to life than a big butt and a smile," Rome sang. He had his Science book in front of him and trying to complete an assignment.

Dre smiled and nodded.

We all agreed.

Chapter 4.

There were girls everywhere at Gee Dub. It seemed, after the conversation with my friends, girls had magically multiplied on campus.

There were freshmen girls, sophomore girls, junior and senior girls walking the halls of Gee Dub. They were short, tall, fat, thin, cute, ugly and everything in between. Gee Dub seemed to teem with girls.

I found myself fascinated by one girl in particular who came to my attention in History class. She, the nameless stranger, sat three desks away and for the first time since I had been at Gee Dub, I noticed her black Kipling backpack, her basketball shoes, her long legs, her tone caramel dipped arms and oval face. That oval face possessed these big eyes and a straight pointed nose above her full lips.

I made it through the beginning of November before I collapsed. Yet, no one noticed. I kept my growing crush hidden. I tried to stay the course, but the heart wants what the heart wants. And of course, I was the first to renege, but no one knew.

At first, I didn't even know. It was as if I was asleep and then awake and this rush of noise and people were all around me. It wasn't that dramatic. It was more like I just found myself paying attention to this unknown girl with the pixie haircut in my History class.

I sat in Mister Troy's class and just listened and took notes and watched the pixie haircut girl with the pouty lips and big eyes. I thought she was cute. No. I thought she was pretty. But I didn't even know her.

So, I waited. I wanted to know the nameless girl, but I didn't dare to ask anyone. I had sworn to avoid girls. So, instead, I watched the girl from afar.

"Yes, Mercedes," Mister Troy said, lowering his black horn-rimmed glasses as was his habit when acknowledging students.

"Mister Troy, I just wanted to know if the marking period project you assigned us can be focused on race and the importance of race on our history."

Mister Troy spent the next ten minutes going back over the marking period project. I secretly laughed at how Mercedes had derailed the lesson with one question. I smiled at Mercedes's ability to throw off men old and Young.

History class ended and right then and there I started thinking of Mercedes. She seemed smart and intense and enticing. Of course, the initial crushing was simple fascination. Mercedes was different. She was interesting.

Now, I was not trying to crush on Mercedes but when I went to Science class, I saw her sitting near the window in the same class with me. I had to do a doubletake. In Science class Mercedes was just two seats away. That was the trick of high school. There were so many things happening at the same time any day.

I tried to fight my thinking about the pixie haircut girl. Yet, there was too much pushing me toward Mercedes. She seemed to be a magnet and I was without warning made of metal shavings and no longer August Manning.

For days, I tried to focus on classwork but every time I walked down the hall or into History or Science class, I looked for Mercedes. The worst part of this desire was it didn't have to be Science or History class for me to hope to catch a glimpse of the straightened black hair on her round head amongst the other students.

At lunch and PE, I tried to get my mind off Mercedes. Dre was trying to manage sophomore math. Will was bored and sullen. Rome was struggling and unusually silent. Lew, the tree hugger, was up in arms about the students not adhering to the recycling.

Me, I was floundering, secretly, and trying to distract myself from Mercedes Copeland. I figured foolishly, if I concentrated on the other girls in my four other classes I might dissuade my mind of the fascination with the curvy Mercedes Copeland.

In Spanish, there was Jasmine, tall and dark and with curly shoulder length hair. She played volleyball and basketball and was a bit of a tomboy. She was cute, but not someone I was interested in except to pick for any PE activities.

Lucy, Hanna and Marsha were three girls in my Math class who seemed attached at the hip. They were best friends since grade school they told everyone. They were a package deal, and I was not interested.

In the same Math class was Shanun, a big boned, brown girl with a bit of an overbite. Shanun was incredibly smart and loved Math. She was also the sister of a local drug boy who was in and out of jail. Shanun was sweet but if you made her list you were on it forever. I liked her but not like that. Shanun was a fighter and I always found myself in Math eavesdropping on who she might have a fight with than really being attracted to the street fighter.

Paris and Faith were in my History and Science class. They were girls but I never considered them anything beyond friends. In History class Faith sat in front of me. Two seats to my right sat Paris. In Science class they were a table away. I knew them from grade school and junior high and realized somewhere after junior high school they, in a flash had become grouped with those potential people of the opposite sex.

In English class there was Terry. She was one of the only girls in my English class who I paid attention to when I was not listening to Mister Whitfield. She had a Coke bottle shape and possessed big brown eyes and full lips, but it was her unconscious biting of her lower lip when trying to figure out things which caught my attention. I sat two rows away from Terry and whenever Mister Whitfield posed a question, I could not help but cut my eyes in her direction. English class was always a success based on how many times I caught Terry nibbling on her bottom lip.

Of the eight girls in my other classes none gave me an iota of attention. Well, that wasn't exactly true. Once or twice, I caught the petite Mercedes Copeland looking at me for no reason and the sight of her looking in my direction made my heart beat a little faster. Mercedes was in two of my six classes. So, twice a day I caught Mercedes Copeland looking my way and smiling or trying not to smile at me and in return I tried not to seem too dorky.

Chapter 5.

September through December

I blinked and the month of August gave way to September. September gave way to Labor Day and then to October. October saw the preparations for Halloween. Though most in Gee Dub publicly did not celebrate Halloween they did dress up for the Halloween contest.

November marked the beginning of basketball practice. I geared up for staying after school four to five days a week. The first few weeks were awkward. When school dismissed daily, I always noticed leaving my last class of the day the school volume was fever pitched for about thirty minutes and then a slight calm fell upon the campus.

During the after-school hours, I ventured forth and, in the calm, found the school chess club and debate club.

A kid with big ears named Bobby oversaw the chess club. The chess club was held in the library and there the twenty boys and girls pushed pieces and prepared for upcoming tournaments. The adult in charge of the chess club was Missus Hawkins, one of the Math teachers. Missus Hawkins was this brilliant woman who had, according to Bobby, been ranked just beneath a Grand Master rating when in college. Auggie knew a Grand Master was the best of the best in chess. No one wanted to play against them.

The debate club was run by Mister Woods, one of the English teachers. He had two whips in charge of the lively club in a junior named Sandra and an intense kid named Colin who were president and vice president. They put everyone through their paces as Mister Woods made sure they were ready for the next debate challenge. I poked my head in and they were debating the commercial sale of military supplies in the nation. It was interesting, but I did not commit to either club. I had other goals in mind.

After school and peeking in on chess or debate I just walked around Gee Dub. It was a spacious place. An hour of wandering about the campus I found the sub-basement where the wrestling team practiced. The coach was a no-neck fireplug of a man I had seen before, but I initially thought was a custodian or vice principal. He was dressed in sweats and gym shoes and slowly torturing a student wearing a T-shirt and gym shorts.

My routine five days a week after school was pretty simple. I checked in with BB and then explored Gee Dub and saw parts of the campus I thought interesting. I would eventually meander back to the gym and work on my homework while BB practiced. In the gym I tried to imagine securing three consecutive honor rolls and gaining my Gee Dub scholar lapel pin while BB and the Gee Dub basketball team did suicides and laps and ran every imaginable play in preparation for their games.

BB in practice was a quiet and attentive leader. He rarely spoke loud enough to hear him from the bleachers. When the coach had the teams break into two teams then BB, my BB appeared.

On offense, he was the floor general. He directed everyone from his high post as the point guard brought the ball up court. BB drew the attention of everyone, and no one could stop him once he touched the ball unless BB decided to pass it to a teammate. He was not a ball hog. He liked passing the ball. Yet, when he got the ball and saw an opening he attacked, and few were able to stop him slashing to the hoop.

On defense, BB was one of the best defenders in the game. He hand checked his opposite and continued to harass the player with the ball. Often BB stole the ball or made his opponent give up the ball sooner than planned.

We had Thanksgiving break. At Gee Dub there was a Thanksgiving assembly in the gym. It was a big production. My freshmen year all of my friends and I laughed and sang and clapped at all the people singing, dancing and performing onstage. It was a great way to end school.

One of the best parts was the Gee Dub teachers performing during the assembly. My freshman year the showstopper had to be the breakdancing performance by one of the gym teachers. People lost their minds. I guess seeing some ancient man pop locking and body rocking was mind blowing. To me, the best part was the windmill Mister Smith did.

We came back after Thanksgiving and prepared for Christmas break. Two weeks later school took a pause for Christmas break. I loved the two weeks off from school. I didn't have to get up early. I didn't have to worry about BB or anyone. All I had to do was wake up, eat, watch TV, play video games and watch movies. Sometimes, during Christmas break, my mom would go to work, and I would be home all alone.

When I was home all alone, I would spend most of the day in my pajamas. I would brush my teeth and wash up and see what was on TV. I might channel surf. I might do nothing. Usually, I would get on my computer and listen to music and turn the volume off on YouTube and watch trending videos.

I loved being lazy. I was not always lazy. I should say I was not always given the opportunity to be lazy. I had lots to do, generally.

During my Christmas break BB was preparing for holiday tournaments and the inevitable beginning of the basketball season. While school was out BB still went to Gee Dub for team practices. He never asked me to go and I never offered.

I spent Christmas with my mom, and we went to my uncle's house and we had Christmas dinner with BB and his baby sister, my cousin Lourdes. Lourdes was this bright and brilliant brat who was too cute for her own good. BB and I gave her a wide berth.

A year younger than me Lourdes did not go to the same junior high. She was special. She was a daddy's girl and had BB's dad wrapped around her twelve-year-old finger.

"Auggie, you like high school," Lourdes asked, her hair expertly straightened to allow part of her hair to cover her round face on her pumpkin head, like she was a prepubescent Aaliyah. I did not answer. Lourdes did not care if I did. She continued on, "I don't know if I want to go to Gee Dub when I finish junior high. I might ask daddy to send me to Royce Academy."

I looked at my spoiled little cousin and smiled. She was dressed in a True Religion sweat top, designer jeans and some new basketball sneakers. Lourdes was everything BB was not.

"Lourdes," I said and as the words came out of my mouth, I regretted saying them. "When was the last time you played basketball?"

Lourdes had a bit of a temper. She narrowed her brown eyes and shot me a look which could have cut me in half with all the heat behind it. The twelve-year-old put a hand on her hip and read me the riot act.

"You know that I don't play sports right now, August Manning. I injured my hip last month and I am on an extended PE rest, if you must know."

I didn't argue. I just surrendered and left Lourdes alone for the remainder of the night.

I walked through the house looking for BB. I found him sitting in the backyard, in the dark.

"What you trying to do become a vampire?"

"What?"

"There ain't no black vampires, BB," I pointed out.

BB shook his head.

I was surprised BB did not correct me. He liked Blade. He had seen all of the movies, even the bad ones. According to BB the Blade trilogy was great. The only bad parts were the characters that were not Blade.

"You okay, BB?"

BB did not answer. He just sat in the dark, quiet. For some reason BB was tense for Christmas break.

"What's wrong," I asked. "You ain't worrying about how many scouts are going to be at the Christmas Hoopala are you? I mean, most scouts ain't going to be there, right? They got families.

They got friends. Only losers would be playing basketball during Christmas break."

"You know Auggie, you are a pain sometimes?"

"But you love me, BB," I countered with a smile. "Family over everything else."

After Christmas break BB started gaining lots of attention from everybody. His skills were on display as the regular season neared. Before the season began everyone was talking about how BB single-handedly helped Gee Dub win the Christmas basketball tournament. There was a New Year's tournament and Gee Dub nearly won the basketball tournament but in the final games' BB was triple teamed. At the Gee Dub versus Jefferson game Mercedes showed up. I could not stop looking at her. It took all my effort to pay attention to what was happening on the court.

She was at the game with some friends, girlfriends, and dressed in a red and black plaid jacket and a black blouse and jeans and black basketball shoes. I know it was crazy but as soon as I saw her, I took all of Mercedes Copeland in from head to toe.

I tore my attention of Mercedes and watched the drama unfold on the court. Jefferson seemed to be willing to double team BB the entire game and force him to beat them with the other four players. It was a crazy game where Jefferson would not allow BB to shine in the finals. BB only scored twenty points and had ten assists and we lost to our city rival 75-70.

Chapter 6.

January- June
Not a Sophomore yet

After we returned from Christmas break, I sat in the same classroom with the caramel dipped beauty and wished I had the courage to say something. I sat in class and tried to come up with the perfect opening. Nothing seemed right. History and Science were tough classes, but they were harder while watching Mercedes Copeland play with her hair or smile or giggle. Unlike the others, Mercedes Copeland had a way of pursing her full lips together and cocking her head to the right or left when trying to understand something, which made me smile.

I didn't like to let my mind wander too much but I thought Lew and Rome had somehow unlocked a combination in my head which had previously been locked and guarded me from being distracted by the opposite sex. I mean, I was only fifteen. Prior to Gee Dub, in junior high, I don't think I really distinguished or cared to distinguish between boys and girls.

The Science class ended, and I watched Mercedes pack up her books and notebooks and slip them into her backpack. She was in no rush. There was no wasted movements I decided. I looked and noticed the class emptying.

"Auggie, you're a mess," Faith said with a roll of her big brown eyes toward Mercedes.

"About what," I said, looking at Faith and Paris looking at me.

"She's out of your league," Paris said looking back in the direction of Mercedes Copeland as Paris slipped on her backpack and pushed by.

I frowned at the back of Paris and looked back at Mercedes gathering her things with her two Afro puffs on her round head.

"She's gonna stomp all over your heart and you ain't even gonna see it coming," Faith said with a sly smile. She shook her head as she prepared to leave Science class and try to catch up with Paris.

I was shocked by Faith's words. No one knew I was secretly crushing on Mercedes Copeland. I was mildly attracted, but I was keeping it mostly in my head.

"What are you talking about?"

"Boys are just so--," Faith stopped herself. She simply shook her head and walked out of class.

I looked back and noticed Mercedes was gone. I walked out of Science class and I ran into Mercedes Copeland just on the other side of the doorway.

"Hi," Mercedes said. Her eyes were big and brown and rested on either side of her diamond-shaped face. Her full lips parted, and the broad smile spread easily across her caramel dipped skin. She tilted her head to the left and studied me.

I muttered something. In speaking I welcomed Mercedes in, like in those old movies with vampires. My destruction was inevitable. The worse part was, I could not tell my friends what was going on. I didn't know what was going on.

"So, you're pretty good in Science," Mercedes said. I nodded. Words escaped me.

"Do you think you can help me with the unit we're working on," Mercedes Copeland asked. I nodded. Again, I didn't know what to say. Mercedes handed me a sheet of paper. I looked down and there was her number. Her number.

"Give me a call," Mercedes said and walked away to her next class.

My high school life turned on those words. "Give me a call." Life before Mercedes was ho hum. Life after Mercedes was in 3-D. It was surround sound. My life was instantaneously, with the receipt of Mercedes Copeland's phone number, like sitting in one of those IMax theaters every day.

The first thing we did was meet at the library. Mercedes got hungry. We went to go eat pizza in the neighborhood.

I don't know what it was about Mercedes but everything I cared about seemed to shrink and become meaningless compared to the pixie haircut girl with the big brown eyes. We held hands. We laughed. We kissed. It amazed me. Secretly, it frightened me a little. I had never found a girl who wanted to hang out with me, who was not in my family. It was unique.

A few days later, we had lunch, and, on the weekend, we went to a movie.

In the defining of the uniqueness, I wanted to hold on to what was peculiarly distinct. Tutoring had morphed into hanging out. Hanging out had shifted to doing things not school related. Then, out of nowhere, we went to a handful of volleyball games since Mercedes liked volleyball. The first time Will and Dre saw us was at a volleyball game.

Will and Dre cornered me after the game.

"What gives man?"

I shrugged.

"You got-got-got a girlfriend?"

"How you not tell us," Will said, a little annoyed.

I did not know what to say. I looked at Will. I looked at Dre. They looked at me.

It seemed we had come to an impasse. I turned to return to Mercedes. Will reached out and grabbed my arm. I turned around, unsure.

"Auggie, be careful," Will warned.

"Yeah, man," Dre said.

"Careful of what?"

Dre shook his head.

"You-you-you don't know-know-know this girl."

"So," I said.

"She's not someone we know," Will said.

"Just be-be-be careful."

Will and Dre looked at me. I nodded. They nodded.

I walked away from Will and Dre and put their negativity on their lack of girlfriends. "Sour grapes" I thought. I learned that term at Gee Dub. Not everyone had my best interest at heart. At least, at that moment, that was how I thought.

I should have listened to Will and Dre. I should have been more cautious, but I wasn't. I wasn't careful at all. I was cocky.

I should have listened to Will and Dre when they warned me about girls I didn't know. All the things I liked about Mercedes began to unravel before my eyes. I felt like I was trying to hold onto smoke. I screwed up everything and Will and Rome had been right.

"BB can I go to the Winter Ball with you and Latoya?"

"What? No. Why," BB asked, as he drove me to school.

"I got a date and I sort of need a little help, you know," I said.

"You got a date?"

"Yeah," I smiled. I hadn't talked to BB about Mercedes for fear of ridicule.

"I heard things, but you know how that goes in high school," BB said letting the Mustang pull us along at its own pace. "I don't put too much stock in the high school grapevine." He paused and looked at me with a strange expression on his brown face. "You messing with someone from the East?"

I shrugged.

"Let me talk to Toy and if she's cool with it. If she's cool then I'm cool with it," BB said. "Did you already buy your tickets?"

I bought tickets to the Winter Ball, knowing it was one of the best high school events of the year. We, BB, Latoya, Mercedes and I, went to the Winter Ball. I wanted to go because I wanted to go with Mercedes. I wanted everyone to see me with the girl with an attitude I had been able to tame long enough to date.

I had rented a tuxedo. Mercedes that night was a sky-blue angel. She was dressed in a sky-blue sequined dress which showed off her delicate shoulders and neck. Her dark hair was loosely piled atop her head with one curlicue of hair loose and dancing above her big brown eyes. She was so beautiful. BB and his date, Latoya Milton, drove with us to the Winter Ball in his rented limousine.

The night had been uneventful. It was just a bunch of kids dressed up and acting like they were going to a movie premiere or a photo shoot. There was loud music. There were lots of people I didn't know. Mercedes and I danced three times. She drifted off and was dancing and laughing with her friends.

BB and Latoya disappeared for a few hours and before the end of the Winter Ball reappeared. They were all giggles and told us they were tired and taking us home. We climbed in the limo and I watched my cousin and Latoya holding hands and kissing. I smiled at Mercedes. Mercedes smiled at me.

The ride back to Mercedes's home was tense. She did not talk or really look at me. I sort of knew things had changed. I just didn't know why.

When she climbed out of the limo it was the last time we smiled or talked or pretended to care about each other.

"Walk her to her door," BB said, with a shake of his head dressed in a white tuxedo and a bright green vest. Latoya, his date, was dressed in a mermaid inspired dress the color of sea foam, all snuggled up against him.

I climbed out of the limo and caught up with Mercedes and she seemed surprised to find me by her side.

"You don't have to walk me to my door," Mercedes said.

"I know, but I want to," I said, looking at her one curlicue of hair loose and dancing on her forehead.

"Well, good night," Mercedes said as she reached her door.

I leaned in and she recoiled. I should have known something was wrong then. She smiled, awkwardly. She hesitantly leaned forward and allowed me to kiss her on the cheek.

I returned to the limo and shrugged Mercedes' weird behavior off. I don't know, I told myself, maybe she was tired after a long night of fun and dancing.

That weekend I made a few calls to see if Mercedes wanted to do anything. I made maybe three calls and as many texts and Mercedes did not text or call back. That was odd, even to me. When I saw her in school Monday, she pretended like I wasn't there.

I waited until after History to confront her in the hallway. People were passing by, on their way to or from class. Some stopped, curious. Other students stopped wanting to watch a little high school drama. I didn't care.

"What's going on?"

"We're done," Mercedes said and with those two words she punctured my bubble of hope I had inflated. It was over.

"What?"

"I don't want to hang out anymore."

"That's it?"

"Yeah, that's it," Mercedes said and shrugged and spun on her heels and walked away.

Chapter 7.

Two dozen and one days

Two dozen and one days was the birth, life and death of my relationship with Mercedes Copeland.

By Science class everyone knew. They were all shaking their heads and giving me the I-told-you-so look. Paris and Faith just rolled their eyes at me anytime I dared look in their direction. In a class of fifty eyes scanning the class and talking and laughing and questioning only two eyes did not pay attention to me and seemed to ignore me the entire class.

I tried to move on but had to admit every time I saw Mercedes there was a slight twinge in the place where she stomped all over my heart. I liked Mercedes. I liked that Mercedes had liked being with me. I missed the ability to just call someone I didn't know, who didn't know me, and talk without fear of them being too busy. When things had been good between Mercedes and me, we could be on the phone for an hour and not even notice.

A few weeks after Mercedes and I were over Faith and Paris still could not help but laugh and giggle at me anytime they caught me casting an eye in the direction of the maneater with a pixie haircut.

"You have to get over her," Faith said.

"There's better girls, Auggie," Paris said, shaking her head.

I tried to not look toward Mercedes too often because every time I did all the memories flooded back to my thoughts. I liked the memory of our first kiss the most. Well, the first kiss and us hugging and holding hands. It was a tie between those two memories.

I would ask to go to the bathroom and when I was out of class I beat myself up mentally. She had broken up with me. She told everyone I was boring. I found out from the whispers and laughs, the hard way, later. That hurt.

I just wanted the school year to end and to get over Mercedes. I hoped the summer would erase all the mistakes I had made my first year at Gee Dub. I secretly just wanted summer to give me time to think of something other than Mercedes.

A week after my first break up there was a freshman Valentine's Day and dance, and I was all alone and depressed. Of course, I did not let anyone know. I hid it expertly.

It is funny how the mind works. While I suffered, I struggled with my own demons. They talked to me over and over, in my head. For a handful of days, at school, I walked around and tried to figure out what I could have done to keep the first girl to kiss me back. Maybe I should have taken her to more places. Maybe, I thought, I should have bought her something. My days at Gee Dub were days filled with hypotheticals and what ifs. When there were quiet moments, I knew everyone was looking at me and thinking of Mercedes' criticism of me as a boyfriend. The worst thing she had said to everyone who would listen was that I was boring.

I sulked. I pouted. It took me sixty days to mope and be a bad friend and to push my loyal friends away from me because I knew they were right, and I didn't want to hear them tell me they were right. In the two months of self-isolation, I tortured myself.

Everyone gave me a wide berth after hearing about me and Mercedes. It was torture. Will, Dre, Lew and Rome saw me but gave me my space. They understood and I hated their understanding.

I went to school every day but did not interact with all the people I considered friends. Before school I did not look for Will or Dre or Lew. At lunch I did not dare go to the lunchroom. I ate my lunch outside on the tennis courts. PE. I wanted to wait until the last moment to arrive and dress out and mope around. I pretended not to see my friends. I was alone.

I dreaded school because everyone knew Mercedes and I were over. Paris and Faith tried to be consoling. In Science class the two tried to give me advice.

"Auggie, she's a climber," Faith said, with a roll of her brown eyes.

"Yeah, she probably was interested in you because you were new or dangerous or bookish," Paris said. "Some girls like that type of guy."

"She might have thought you were cuckoo," Paris said spinning her forefinger by her temple. "You know how everyone thought you were," she paused. "At the beginning of the year."

"Not us," Faith said with a scowl.

"No, we know you are," Paris began only to stop, trying to find the right words. "You are a puppy, and we are looking for a pit bull and not chihuahua."

"I just--," I cut myself off. I didn't want to share.

"My mom told me that girls in high school are only looking for one of two things," Paris said. "You know the first one. The other is protection." Paris looked at me sadly. "I suppose she figured you were the third option."

"What's that?"

"Comedy? I don't know."

"Yeah, I know girls like her," Faith said with a laugh.

I nodded. I didn't agree. I couldn't agree. At least, not then.

"Well, anyway, you are better off without her," Faith said.

"She's only looking to use people," Paris said.

I listened not because I thought either one was correct. I listened because they were in the same class and I could not get up and walk out. Sometimes, it was easier to weather the storm in the little hut than run out into the storm and face the rain and the wind.

Every day I had to see Mercedes in History class and Science class. It was like being shot and stabbed and not being stupid enough to pass out or give into the pain and then be shot and stabbed again over and over every time I looked at her. Just when I thought all the pain might subside, I would go two classes without seeing her and then walk into Science and feel the whole shooting and stabbing all over again for fifty minutes.

My sanctuary, the lunchroom table with my friends vanished. I could not drag myself to the lunchroom when my friends were there. I sat in the gym for lunch and became one of those weird kids in high school with no friends. I had been banished and no one had to tell me I was banished. I had imposed it on myself. My friends didn't say anything. They didn't scream at me. They weren't angry. They just did not engage and that made it exponentially hard to overcome. In my confusion I felt I had disappointed Mercedes and betrayed my friends. I was a horrible person.

During my exile basketball season ended. BB had an impressive senior year. The team though did not and after winning the district championship over Jefferson Gee Dub was bounced by a team from the city in the first round to the state championship.

Without Gee Dub in the run to the championship school returned to the semblance of normalcy. I went to class. I sulked. I pouted. I avoided everyone who cared about me.

With basketball over BB would pick me up and drive me home every day after school. He must have known about me and Mercedes but to his credit he never said anything. We just drove and listened to music and enjoyed the Mustang.

As I sat in the Mustang with BB driving me home after school, I realized I would have my fourteenth birthday in social isolation. My birthday never was a big deal generally, but that year it was an even less significant event without Will, Rome, Dre or Lew acknowledging my presence. I didn't expect them to do anything. In the past, they might buy a card or make a card.

My fourteenth birthday I didn't expect anything. I wasn't disappointed. Well, I was a little disappointed because no one from the group even looked at me on my birthday.

Therefore, I avoided anyone who might care to talk to me. In class I became a one-word answerer. I fell deeper into my depressed spiral.

One day, Mister Davenport stopped me in the hall. It was a strange exchange. I had been cleared of worrying by Davenport the first semester. I was sane. I was a normal, confused teenager. Davenport wrote a glowing report on my stability. I remember my mom got the report and let me read it. There were lots of scientific things and psychological doublespeak. The thing I recalled was the final statements. *"August is a very respectful teenager. He wants to succeed. He is, like many his age, trying to come to grips with who he is and his purpose. He is no threat to himself or others. He possesses a keen mind and a good heart."*

"You okay, August?" Mister Davenport checked in once a week and noted my change in behavior. One of the teachers had recommended me to Davenport.

"Yes," I said. I could not look at Mister Davenport. I felt he would see my anger and think I was going to harm myself. That thought was the furthest thing from my mind. I was struggling with the concept of friendship. I had in one action betrayed one group of friends for the attention of someone else. It was such a maddening situation.

"I was told by Mister Troy you were having some social issues and I should check in with you," Davenport smiled. "So, I'm checking in. You okay?"

All around us students I had known and who knew me eavesdropped and smiled and cut their eyes in my direction. There were no familiar faces in the passing groups of people to save me from Davenport and his concern. I didn't know if I had seen those I betrayed if I would have accepted their saving at that moment. I deserved everything I was getting. At least, that was how I felt. So, I stood and looked at Mister Davenport's polished brown leather lace-up dress shoes.

I nodded. I had no answer. I found myself confused about the whole two dozen and one days with Mercedes.

"August, you know you can talk to me anytime you need?" Davenport's words snapped me out of my mental spiral.

"I'm fine. I just have a lot on my mind."

"Like what?"

"Well, things. High school things. Grades and all," I said, still not looking at Mister Davenport. People were passing by. They were looking at me. They seemed to always be looking at me since the break-up. "You know. High school stuff."

"Well, if you need any help with those high school things you should know that I went to high school and understand that high school stuff more than you might know."

I looked up the hall and saw kids thinning. I figured classes were about to start. I didn't want to be late. That was my excuse. That would get me out of this awkward conversation with Mister Davenport.

"Can I go? I don't want to be late."

"Sure," Mister Davenport said. "If you are late come to my office and I'll write you a pass."

I ran to class. I ran from Mister Davenport. I ran toward my next class and didn't know what to do. I decided I had to put on a happy face. I didn't want my teachers ratting me out to Mister Davenport. I didn't need that kind of attention.

Mister Davenport told me early about people who were traumatized and how they dealt with trauma. Denial was the most common. I decided to go with the most common way to deal with my own trauma.

My grand plans at Gee Dub melted away to a day-to-day high school experience. I still held onto the desire to be a Gee Dub scholar. If nothing else, that goal was still intact.

Every day was divided into seven hours at school. Every week was thirty-five hours of school. A month was twenty days of school. Seven hundred hours plus or minus depending on holidays. (I did the math.)

For the remainder of the school year, I kept my head down and concentrated on things I should have done before Mercedes Copeland. Classwork and homework gave me purpose. In class I could succeed. With my homework I proved my worth. Yet, every day I went to school, under my self-imposed banishment, I did not feel comfortable when I saw my understanding four friends.

Once, I was in the hall and thinking about what Davenport said when I saw Will and Lew heading toward me. They were talking and laughing and hadn't noticed me. I slipped inside the closest office, the counseling office.

It wasn't a passing period, and classes were going on, and no one was in the small office. I sat and waited and watched the window for Will and Lew to pass. While in the counselor's office I picked up one of the College Planning magazines and pretended to read it waiting for my friends to pass.

My life became a joke. I was hiding from my friends because of a girl. My desire to be with a girl had broken up the friendships I had built up in nearly half of my life and it was all my fault. It was a tough realization.

I took the College Planning magazine and put it in my backpack and thought nothing of it when I left the empty counseling office. I returned to class and did not run into Will and Lew or anyone on my way back to class.

School kept moving forward despite my guilt and inability to stand up and talk to my friends. I made the honor roll for the fourth time, but still not three in a row, and was aware I would receive my Gee Dub scholar lapel pin if I got on the honor roll the next marking period. Without my friends I plowed on.

Having screwed up socially, I focused on my classwork and homework. My textbooks, homework and notebooks, were my friends in lieu of no friends at all.

The constant in all this turmoil was BB. My superstar of a cousin checked in, but never pushed. He had to know what had happened. Gee Dub wasn't that big a school. Students talked. Yet, BB never brought up Mercedes or where she was, even though we had all gone to the Winter Ball together. Perhaps, the most telling thing was that Latoya did not say anything about Mercedes when she saw me.

Chapter 8.

Two times BB surprised me my freshman year. The first was a
couple of weeks after my birthday. I climbed in the Mustang one
Thursday morning, and to my surprise there a gift-wrapped present
sitting on my seat.

"What's this?"

"I forgot about your birthday, you know, during the season,
and I wanted to make up for it and get you something," BB said with
a wry smile.

I smiled too. I thought it was a prank. BB had a sick sense of
humor. He thought that fart jokes were hilarious. He liked watching
those old school variety shows. He liked those screwball comedies.
All I had to do was mention "White Girls" and he would tell me how
the movie was one of his favorites.

"Thanks, I think," I said putting the box gingerly on the floor
and climbing in.

"Open it," BB said with a big smile.

I looked at BB, skeptically, he was smiling from ear-to-ear.
For all I knew it could be a hot steaming pile of dog poop inside the
box. Or a rat. Or a rat sitting on a pile of hot steaming dog poop.

"This ain't a prank is it?"

"Naw, open it up," BB said as we sat in the Mustang.

I opened the box and was surprised to find a new pair of
Nike basketball sneakers. I pulled one of the shoes out and
examined it. The shoe was one of the newest Air Jordans in black
and red.

"Thanks," I smiled.

BB nodded. BB let the Mustang nose into the street. We
drove through the streets and that morning I admired my new
shoes.

"Thanks," I said again, feeling my smile spread across my face. It had been a long time since I had smiled organically, I thought. "I really appreciate the shoes."

BB nodded. He drove on and at a stop light he turned and looked at me holding my shoes.

"I'm good," I lied.

BB let it go. He had other things on his mind. He was trying to decide which college he was going to attend.

By the middle of April, my cousin BB, who was inundated with college acceptance letters and life decisions, called me to come over to his house. It was Saturday. I should have known something was up. I could have counted on my one hand all the times Benaiah Benning Jr. called me.

BB was my ride to school. We were family but once we arrived at school, he rarely acknowledged me even though we went to the same high school. It wasn't intentional. It was just the fact BB was a senior and preparing to graduate and I was a lowly freshman, still wet behind the ears.

"How come you can't come get me?"

"My car isn't working right now. Come on by, you know you ain't doing nothing. Call me when you are on the bus," BB said and ended the conversation.

BB lived a bus ride away from my house. My mom wasn't home. If she was, I might have asked her for a ride. Reluctantly, I checked the weekend schedule and headed to the bus stop. I texted BB as I got comfortable on the bus.

The ride was scenic. The AC Transit headed back toward downtown and at the light, before the freeway, turned left and left again and headed toward the Oakland hills. The bus was not too crowded as we made our way up a slight hill toward the richer neighborhoods. Ahead another freeway separated the lowlands from the higher rent areas. I pressed the stop request button and the nearly empty bus slowed and stopped just three blocks from the freeway which went to the other side of the hills.

My uncle Benaiah and aunt Arna lived on the border of two parts of the city. Above them, in the hills were the million-dollar homes. Below them, just ten blocks away, were low rent apartments. I tried to think if I could fly, I could cut across the twenty or thirty blocks separating my house on MacArthur from my uncle's comfortable home below the Mormon Temple.

My uncle worked for a cable company. He was a higher up and had been there for years. His work afforded their house and three cars. It sat on a small hill just about five minutes from the closest bus stop. The house was a big ranch style home with a big front yard. BB always complained he had to cut the grass every week during the warm months.

As I walked up to the house I noted, sitting in the driveway, BB's blue Mustang. I wondered why BB did not pick me up? I climbed up the three steps to the small front porch and rang the doorbell. I turned and looked at the quiet street where the house sat. There was no one outside.

My cousin opened the front door and smiled. His big eyes and big ears were the first thing I saw.

As BB reached out and put a big hand on the door jamb, I could not help but take in his gigantic hands. BB was dressed in a T-shirt, basketball shorts and basketball sneakers.

"What's up, little man," BB said. He looked over my shoulder but didn't move or break his composure.

I smirked at BB. I looked back at the Mustang.

"How come you didn't pick me up?"

BB shook his head and smiled. He was otherworldly up close. He was incredibly tall compared to me. Everything seemed exaggerated. He looked like one of those elongated brown boy cartoon characters from Jacob Lawrence with a close fade to me.

"I told you. The 'stang is down for a minute." He ushered me in and before I could speak, he continued talking as he led me to the kitchen. "Come on. I hear you broke up the band. Over a girl. I just found out, sort of and you suddenly find yourself a man, well boy, without a country. Or in your case, without friends."

"BB, why did you ask me over, to talk about the obvious? How are we getting to school Monday?"

"Don't worry about my car, right now," BB said with a smile and turned and walked back toward the kitchen. I followed, annoyed. BB walked through the living room and into the kitchen. There, in the kitchen, sat Will, Rome, Dre and Lew at the table. I froze.

"Come in, Auggie," BB said.

"Damn, man, look-look-look at him," Dre laughed.

"He looking like he done seen a ghost," Lew said elbowing Rome.

"You can't say, Hi?" Will said.

Rome just smirked.

I lowered my head. I wanted to turn around and leave.

BB put a big hand on my shoulder. He was smiling. I looked at his toothy grin and back at the four in the kitchen. He turned and said, "Lew, thought this would be a good thing."

I looked to Lew, who was smiling like he had won the Nobel Peace Prize.

I shook my head.

All four just sat and smiled. I felt awkward. I wanted to turn around and go back out the front door. Though I knew everyone in the kitchen I felt exposed.

"You guys grew up together and you can't let your stupid emotions and hormones screw all that up, Auggie," BB said.

I winced at the accusation. I knew BB was right. I sort of squirmed.

No one spoke.

"You guys are the Jackson Five or The Incredibles or I don't know," BB said, searching for famous groups of five.

"Who's Jermaine and Tito," Rome smiled.

"Who's Jack Jack," Lew joked.

"I al-al-always saw us mo-mo-more as the Power Rangers," Dre smiled.

"You the pink one," said Rome with a smirk.

"Screw you," Dre hissed.

"That ain't very Power Ranger-like," Lew said.

Dre pouted. Rome punched Dre in the shoulder. Dre punched Rome back.

"Drop all that. We all came here to squash this stupid stuff," Will spat.

Dre, sitting next to Will, frowned at Rome. Rome all smiles thought the back and forth was just playing. Rome opened his hands and raised them in surrender.

I looked at Will and everyone in the kitchen and felt terrible. Will was my oldest friend. We had been friends since the second grade. Rome and Dre had been my friends since third grade. Lew had become my friend in sixth or seventh grade, when he moved to Oakland, from Louisiana, with his family.

"So, how do we decide if we can trust him?"

"He's a definite flight risk," Will said to Lew.

"Definite," repeated Dre.

"Can't trust 'em," Lew said.

I wasn't sure if Lew was talking about me or girls or what.

"Well, if we were a street gang, we could jump him in," Rome said.

"We're not a street gang," Dre managed.

"We're not jumping Auggie in," Lew said.

"So, what's your suggestion?"

"I figured he would come and apologize, and we would just move on."

"I don't know if everyone would be cool with that," Rome said.

I listened. We all had good times and bad times. I had fought with each person sitting at the table. Yet, I loved them all. They were my best friends.

BB stepped into the kitchen proper. The fighting subsided. BB stepped to the refrigerator and opened it and pulled out a bottled water.

"They didn't have to come," BB said. He stepped back to the entrance to the kitchen and leaned on the counter.

"I have to be honest," Rome began. "I didn't want to come to this. Will sort of forced me."

Will smiled at Rome's words. I smiled too. I could just see Will literally twisting Rome's arm to make him come to BB's house.

"I'm-I'm-I'm going to say what-what-what everyone is thinking," Dre stuttered. "Was she worth-worth-worth it?"

I lowered my eyes. I didn't want to say no, but I didn't want to say yes either. Mercedes Copeland had been nice, at first. She was all cute and pretty and sweet smelling. Then she changed. It didn't take long. After the Winter Ball things just went off the rails.

I shook my head, dejected. I had betrayed my friends. The worse part was I betrayed them for a girl. I wanted to apologize to everyone.

"It's too late for all that now," Will said, with a smirk and shake of his head. His words brought me back to the kitchen with my lifelong friends.

"I'm sorry," I breathed.

"We passed that." Will paused. "I was two minutes from axing this whole friendship thing."

"Me too," said Dre.

Everyone looked at Will and Dre and then back to me. No one spoke.

"I'm sorry," I repeated a little louder. "I messed up."

The four looked at each other and then at me. Dre smirked. Rome scowled. Lew licked his lips, like he was hungry. Will studied me quietly.

"So," Lew said, breaking the silence which had built up. "We good?"

"I don't know," I said.

"Yeah, I don't think we're good. We will be more like the Four Musketeers for now. We will be watching you, Auggie," Rome said, with a smirk. "We know you're a flight risk."

"Yeah, you-you-you are like D'ar-D'ar-D'artagnan," Dre smiled, and patted me on the shoulder.

"Yeah, we know where your loyalty is," Lew said.

Rome climbed to his feet and faked like he was going to punch me.

"With-with-with a big butt and a smile," Dre laughed.

BB kicked us all out after making us all do his chores as a payment for sort of solving my banishment. When we left things were not magically resolved. Rome did not seem fazed one way or the other. Lew was unmoved. Dre seemed okay. Will and BB were skeptical. Well, everyone was skeptical. I was a risk to everyone I considered friends.

Chapter 9.

Still not a Sophomore

The remaining two months of my freshmen year were spent trying to rebuild relations I had destroyed. Mercedes Copeland moved on with her life. I heard through the Gee Dub grapevine she was dating a junior named Franco.

In May, BB announced to the world his decision to go to one of the top ten basketball programs in the nation. His announcement merited TV coverage and several newspaper reporters discussing his decision. The college basketball coach had flown out and appeared at the signing of the letter of intent. BB's signing was a big deal.

It was a nice moment for BB. He had worked hard to secure his athletic scholarship. His parents were so proud. Hell, I was proud, and I was just his cousin.

We went to dinner at Red Lobster and celebrated BB's signing. Latoya, his girlfriend, was there as well. It was a great night.

At school things kept moving toward the end of the year. Lew, Dre and Rome seemed to accept me back into their good graces. Will though was a hold out. Nothing I did could break through his defenses. He was not hostile, but he was not friendly either. It was a bit frustrating.

I gave him time. I had the Gee Dub Scholar lapel pin on my radar. I was so close.

Time sped up after BB's signing. School and all the drama of school shrank. Spring break was a week away. After Spring break, we took our finals. So, at the end of March we prepared for upcoming tests.

A few days before the shortened weeks of school Will sat at the lunch table and quite as a matter of fact retold us a fantastic story, he heard in his Science class.

"I was in Science class and, you know, on short days, he usually shows science videos. We watch these newsclips and then write about them for grades."

"We know how school works, Will," Rome said.

"Anyway, today he showed this video of this bird that usually lives on the east coast and this bird, I can't remember the name of it, somehow," Will paused, thinking. "I think there was a hurricane or El Nino or something and when all the other birds headed south this one bird found itself flying west."

"So," Dre said, bored.

"So, the bird flew with the help of these winds, or something, 3,000 miles and landed on the west coast. It is a kind of crazy story because it is the only bird from that species now on the west coast. It's all by itself on the west coast."

"What?" Dre, Lew and Rome said in unison.

"Yeah," Will said with a giant smile on his brown face. "It's flying around San Francisco."

Almost immediately, I had a million questions.

"When did this happen?" Rome asked.

"Can the bird get back to its own kind?" Lew asked.

"What kind of bird is it," I asked.

"How-how-how come no other birds like it live-live-live here," Dre asked.

It seemed Will's story ignited questions from Lew, Rome and Dre.

"Where can I see this story," I asked Will, the sudden center of attention at our lunch table.

"Man, I don't know all that stuff," Will confessed. "I kind of found the story crazy. That's why I'm telling you about it."

"Are they going to do anything to get the bird back to its own kind?" Lew asked.

"Man, I said I don't know," Will said and climbed to his feet and went to get his lunch.

"That is one cra-cra-crazy story," Dre stammered.

"Well, it is unique," I said. "I mean, everyone is interested."

Well, everyone was interested except Will. I chalked it up to he and me having the falling out. We had fought before. It was nothing new. He had expectations of me. I had expectations of him. Sometimes we got upset for whatever reason and needed some time apart. At least, that was how I saw it on the other side of Mercedes Copeland and trying to get the team back together.

Will would come around, I thought. He had to. What choice did he have?

The story of the lost bird fascinated me. There was just so much about the story I didn't know, and those missing parts held my attention. After hearing the story, I did a little research and in my light attempt to find out some more information I found nothing on a lost bird in the Bay Area. It wasn't surprising. A lot of the news was written for certain audiences.

As school wound down and my freshman year ended, I went to see Mister Johnson. I wanted to see that video. We were on half days the last week of school and most teachers were showing movies or having classroom parties. During English class I left and decided to catch up with Mister Johnson. I didn't have him as a teacher but being a Gee Dub scholar made me notable. His room was not too far from my English class and when I got to his room the door was open. I walked in like I owned the place. He seemed a little surprised to see me in his classroom.

Mister Johnson was a dusky brown, short haired, square faced man with a beard and mustache and wire rimmed glasses and a pot belly. He looked to be fifty at least. He was dressed in light blue polo shirt, belt and slacks. He was packing up his room when I stuck my head in his room. Johnson smiled at me, like my mom did when I said something profound.

"What can I do for you, young man?"

"I dipped out to talk to you," I said. I had my hands in my pants pockets.

"You're... August Manning," Johnson said, straightening out and studying me. He was maybe six foot tall, I guessed. He seemed to favor his right leg for some reason.

I nodded.

"August, you're not one of my students," Mister Johnson began.

"I know Mister Johnson," I said. "But you know me. I also thought that being at George Washington Carver every teacher was a teacher for every student in and out of class," repeating what the principal had said over and over to students and parents and teachers as well.

"Okay, August," Mister Johnson conceded. "How can I help you?"

"Well, Mister Johnson, school is almost over, and Will, William Hutchinson, told me that you showed a video about some lost bird." I paused, letting what I said sink in.

Johnson blinked and nodded. The apprehension and uncertainty on his face a second before vanished. He relaxed just a little.

"Well, I was wondering if one, I could see the video, and two, I was hoping you could give me some more information?"

Mister Johnson looked around his quiet room. I had come to see him the last period of the day. He could have told me to beat it. He could have said no. Mister Johnson did neither.

"You know, you caught me packing up my room," the teacher said, with a gap-toothed smile.

I nodded. I looked and saw the work he had done. There were several boxes sitting on desks, half packed. I assumed it was all his personal stuff he was taking home.

"Give me a moment to pull up the video," Mister Johnson nodded and smiled.

He gestured to a desk and I sat down. He pressed a few buttons on his desktop computer on his desk and the LED projector bolted to the ceiling blinked on.

"It's not very long. You need me to turn off the lights?"

"Naw," I grunted.

I watched the video while Mister Johnson continued to pack. The science video was only about seven minutes and the bird portion was only about three minutes long.

Just like Will had described it the video laid out this lost bird that had somehow crossed from the Atlantic Ocean to the Pacific Ocean. There were three scientists that had theories on how the bird made it over three thousand miles across the United States, but none seemed convinced. Much of the video was bird watchers camped out with binoculars and cameras. They weren't scientists, just enthusiasts. The two bird watchers who first reported the gannet were interviewed. They were bird enthusiast famous unexpectedly. Then, finally, there was a video of a bird flying in the air near some cliff faces. The bird looked like a seagull. Well, the closer I looked the less it looked like a seagull. It had black shoulders and a black tail. That was unusual.

The video ended.

I climbed out of the desk and thanked Mister Johnson. Mister Johnson was in the back of his room packing his books from a bookshelf next to his desk.

"Those your personal books?"

"They are," Mister Johnson smiled.

"You need some help?"

Mister Johnson stopped his packing and studied me. I could hear the wheels in motion in his head. The way I saw it there were only two responses: yes or no.

"I'm good, August, thanks for asking." He paused and smiled again. "Why did you want to see the video?"

"I was curious. Will, William, got really excited about the whole lost bird thing."

He nodded and smiled. "Yeah, it was a big hit in class. A lot of people were surprised something like that could happen." Mister Johnson paused. "Science is always finding itself scrambling to explain the unexplainable." Johnson smiled and looked at me looking at him. "You need anything else?"

"Well, remember I did ask you for some more information on the bird," I said, with a slight smile.

"I don't know that much about it. What little I do know I placed on the desk, while you were watching the video. That's all I got."

I nodded.

"Anything else?"

"No, well, I was just curious why you picked that video," I said. I knew he was the Science teacher and all but my Science teacher, Mister Ross, hadn't shown the bird video.

"Well, one of the teachers recommended it," Mister Johnson said. "It's the weirdest thing."

I smiled.

"I think he secretly wanted to be a bird guy, but things worked out and he became a computer teacher," Mister Johnson said more to himself.

"Who's that?"

"You know Mister Pope?"

I didn't. I thanked Mister Johnson again and grabbed the papers he gave me. After school I ran into Lew.

"Mister Pope," I said to Lew with a big smile on my face.

"Who's that?"

"I don't know," I said.

"Then why are you all smiling like you won the lottery?"

"I suppose because there's someone else interested in this bird," I said.

Lew shook his head.

"Auggie, just because you got a name don't mean much," Lew said. "I mean, there's how many teachers here?"

"I don't know," I said.

"Right, I don't know either, but there are a bunch of them and not all of them teach freshmen classes or sophomore classes. I'm just saying not to get your hopes up too high on this magical teacher being our savior."

"I ain't saying nothing like that," I said.

"I'm just saying."

"I'm just saying."

Chapter 10.

With just a couple of days before the last day of school I tried to find Mister Pope. No luck. I asked my advisory teacher, Miss Bruin. That was a mistake. She was a pie-faced woman in her fifties who had been at Gee Dub since it started, some said. I doubted that. She loved to talk. She had a story for every question asked. After five minutes Miss Bruin forgot what we were talking about and told me to go back to my seat.

Then it was three days before BB graduated. I was surprised when he called me and told me to go for a drive with him. He picked me up and I climbed into the Mustang and we took a drive. It was unusual for BB to want to do anything with me. So, immediately I was on guard. I knew something was up but could not guess what that something was.

The BB driving was an extremely serious BB. He seemed borderline sad, but I had never really seen my cousin sad. I wanted to ask him if he was okay, but we didn't really do that. BB was this high school superstar and untouchable personality who had it all together. He had signed to a top ten basketball program which had gone to the Final Four in the last four years. BB should have been the happiest person in the Mustang. He wasn't.

We drove for a full ten minutes with the music playing loud in the car, but without BB saying anything. I just sat in the passenger seat and watched the world go by. BB's Mustang was one of those Mustangs with the throwback Mach V body and was loud and angry anytime he pushed the gas. BB that night did not drive on the freeway, instead he drove through the surface streets toward the hills.

The drive was not faster, but it was more colorful. We stopped at a light and watched as a homeless man with a sign started panhandling. I looked at BB who usually gave the panhandlers a hard time. He had this weird look on his face. It was a cross between sadness and anger. I wasn't sure if he was going to curse the man out approaching the Mustang or give him one hundred dollars.

Before the man could reach the car, the light changed, and BB pulled away. I didn't say anything. I just kept watching BB out of the corner of my eye. He looked likely to do anything.

We were in the beginning of the foothills and I was going to point out the zoo which was only a turn away but chose not to say anything. BB wouldn't have listened. BB drove past the zoo entrance and into the hills. As we started to climb into the hills BB finally spoke.

"You know sometimes when you are working so hard for one thing you start to miss the most important things happening all around you," BB said.

I sat in the Mustang and tried to figure out what BB was talking about.

"Yeah," I said, not knowing what my cousin was talking about, but enjoying the ride in the hills of the nearby city I only looked at from my home.

"Don't forget the most important things, Auggie," BB said as we drove through the dark streets and weaved our way to the top of the hill. "I mean, think about what's important. Make that your goal. But while you're heading for that goal don't let the little things pass you by."

"BB, what are you talking about?"

"Life, man," BB said. He steered the Mustang across the crest of the hill where the rich people lived. I looked at the big houses and the big gates and the expensive cars in the driveways. BB slowed and we slowly drove into a school which sat on the skyline. The parking lot was open, and BB found a parking spot which overlooked the city below. The nighttime view was spectacular. I had never been to the hills and to the parking lot. I did not imagine there was a view like this to see the city below.

"Remember Auggie, you decide your path," BB said. "Don't let people who don't have dreams decide your path or direction."

I listened. I didn't disagree. For some reason just being near BB was enough. I didn't have to answer. BB was the talker that night. I was the thinker.

"BB," I said as he drove me back to my house. "You know Mister Pope?"

"Yeah, why?"

"Curious. Is he cool people?"

"He is. He don't play. He's cool and all but don't take his kindness for softness."

I climbed out of the Mustang and BB drove away.

A couple of days later I went to BB's graduation. It was held in the auditorium of the small all women's college just on the other side of the town. It reminded me of one of those theaters where comedians perform. It was crowded and people milled about just like at a basketball game, except with nicer clothes.

My mom and I got BB a money necklace. I walked to BB before graduation and gave him the lei.

"Thanks, little... Auggie," BB smiled. He showed two gold canine teeth. I shook my head at the sight. BB was always so buttoned up, but when he could he tried to be like everyone else. The gold canine's wasn't a gold grill. It was subtle, like BB. My cousin was always doing something to show people he was just like them but at the same time not like everyone else.

"Proud of you, man," I managed to say before the graduation started. He nodded. I smiled and spun on my heels.

As I walked back to my seat, I saw Latoya, but she seemed preoccupied. She was on her phone.

After graduation we went to a restaurant and celebrated BB's accomplishment.

My last report card of the school year announced I made the honor roll for the sixth time out of eight attempts and received my Gee Dub scholar lapel pin. There was a fancy note sent to me from Mister Allen himself. The note said I would receive my lapel pin by mail, over the summer.

I didn't show anyone my report card or the note at the lunch table. I was still a little tender about the whole Mercedes thing and did not want my friends to use my brain and success against me.

The way I saw it, things were just getting back to normal. I didn't need to rub their noses in the fact I received the Gee Dub scholar lapel pin.

School ended. Summer began. My life was for most of June helping BB pack for college. He seemed happy and a little nervous to go to the middle of nowhere and play basketball.

"You know that there is all this hype all of a sudden about me leaving," BB said, one afternoon when we were sitting in his backyard. He was wearing his basketball shorts and a professional basketball jersey. Under the jersey was a short sleeve T-shirt. On his feet BB was wearing Nike slides.

"It's a big deal," I said. "I mean, most people stay in state. I mean, you are going to Kansas." I paused. "I don't know nobody that has gone to Kansas on purpose."

BB laughed. It was nice to hear my cousin laugh. This side of BB few saw. He was all of a sudden relaxed and comfortable.

"I can see that," BB smiled.

He cut the grass in the backyard. I helped him edge the yard. We raked the grass trimmings and bagged them.

"You know I'm leaving next month," BB said. "I get the summer educational orientation."

"I think that is good," I said, not knowing what BB needed to orient himself to in Kansas.

At the beginning of the summer before I became a sophomore, I got a small package from school. I opened it and showed my mom my gold-plated Gee Dub scholar lapel pin. We reveled in the achievement. She knew what it took to receive one of the lapel pins.

"I'm proud of you, baby," she said. "I will look for something to celebrate your moment."

A few days later my mom surprised me with a fashionable gray blazer which was a little big for me.

"You will grow into it," my mom said with a smile.

I slipped it on and for a few moments all the silliness of the school year fell away. I loved my blazer. It was my first blazer. I examined it and found out it was made by an Italian designer I never heard of, but that wasn't saying much. I thanked my mom over and over for the blazer.

The next day I went to the neighborhood cleaner and had my blazer dry cleaned. It was the first thing I ever dry cleaned.

A few days before BB left for college, he gave me his new college number and told me to text him if I needed advice. Of course, I didn't plan on texting BB for advice. I didn't really need advice. I just appreciated the idea of BB being just a text message away.

Chapter 11.

Sophomore Summer

Before I became a sophomore, the team broke up for the summer. Lew went to stay with his father on the other side of town for the summer. It was an arrangement his mother and father had. Dre did a road trip every summer with his parents. They were headed to New Orleans for some reason. Dre said they had family there. Rome went to New York for the summer. The only person of the four to stay in town was Will, but he was still not talking to me. It was odd, but not unusual for Will to hold a grudge. So, I just waited him out. I figured I would give him the summer and when school started back force him to be my friend like the old days.

For two months I lounged around the house or walked around the neighborhood. I think I went to the public swimming pool maybe four or five times. Once, I went to the local park and shot some hoops in a pick-up game. I was horrible. I had fun and no one picked me for the rest of the day.

In the quiet of my home, in my bedroom, while my mom was at work, I crafted a plan to gain the most scholarships possible and a genuinely unique idea to gain the attention of all the colleges I intended to apply for my senior year at Gee Dub.

A few days before the start of school I had the bare bones of a plan sketched out. To see if the plan was possible, I had to talk to my counselor and decide what community activity would garner enough attention to make colleges pay attention.

Now, I could have been selfish and only thought of myself, but I had done that and nearly destroyed friendships I cared about. So, the first person I told was my mom.

"Auggie, this is only your sophomore year, baby," she said. "Don't you think that you are jumping the gun, a little?"

I tried to explain the idea. She listened. In the end, she did as she always did. She encouraged me.

"I think that you are incredibly talented Auggie," my mother said. "If you put your mind to it, I cannot see how you don't succeed."

"Thanks ma," I said.

In my mind I was excited and heading into my sophomore year at Gee Dub. Sixty days gave teenagers amnésia. In those sixty days teens swept all the good and bad things under the rug and out of their minds for thoughts of summer. At least, that was my thinking.

So, I laid low and read and did my research on the lost bird. I sat on roof and watched the clouds and skimmed the short article Mister Johnson had given me about the bird. It was just a portion of a longer article from the Chronicle. I grabbed my laptop computer and did a little more research.

I discovered there were three articles about the wayward bird which defied all odds somehow and crossed from the Atlantic to the Pacific. I read all of them.

The first article was from a small island paper called the Farrallon Forum. It was just two paragraphs which stated several bird watchers were on a bird watch and observed a gannet flying near the cliffs. But the problem, the bird watchers argued amongst themselves, was there being three types of gannets in the world. None of the gannets were native to the Pacific. There was a big debate of the bird watchers of the authenticity of the gannet sighting. The handful of bird watchers tried to photograph the mysterious bird.

There were only two photographs which showed any detail of the winged anomaly. Of the dozens of shots only six photographs were good, but the markings were hard to distinguish. The bird was black and white but decidedly too small to be a gannet they decided. Most suggested the bird in question looked like a big seagull.

A week later, a second article, from a bigger paper, was published. The article was in the Half Moon Bay Log. Again, there were bird watchers who identified the gannet as a seagull and been skeptical of the sightings. There were three local bird watchers who believed they found the first gannet on the Pacific West. Most bird watchers laughed at the idea.

The next time the errant bird winged along the cliffs they had cameras capturing the big bird's flight. It was the second set of nearly twenty photographs which silenced all doubters. There were fourteen clear pictures of the Northern Gannet. The Northern Gannet or *Morus bassanus* was a seabird, the largest of the gannet family *Sulidae*.

The biggest article came from the San Francisco Chronicle. The difference in the Chronicle article was the depth of the questions and the sheer number of experts weighing in on the unexpected Pacific visitor. The reporter took the time to consult with bird experts.

The Chronicle article mentioned the information from the two other articles but more. The articles, including the Chronicle, were vague in how the Northern Gannet got from the east coast to the west coast. The scientists who offered theories did not know for sure. All they knew was somehow the gannet was now flying around three points on the west coast.

The Chronicle, online, featured all twenty-six pictures in the article. I clicked them and studied them.

Mo was a handsome fellow. He had this elegance in the picture which caught him mid-flight. There seemed to be determined and regal character to the bird and an intelligence or sadness in his big black eyes.

Almost immediately I wanted to figure out a way to the Farrallon Islands or Half Moon Bay. Of course, getting to either was impossible without a car. BB was gone. He was in the middle of nowhere and I was on MacArthur Boulevard, next to the EBMUD sump station and an abandoned warehouse. I liked it because my closest neighbor was across the street above the post office or the ballroom where they held the traditional and nightlong celebrations for Latin girls turning fifteen. I loved hearing the laughter and singing to accordion music almost weekly for the endless

Quinceaneras. At the corner was the 7-11 store which I went to now and then, but never after dark.

I did my research and if I took only public transit, I could not get to the Farrallon Islands. Half Moon Bay was impossible as well. I found a Greyhound bus which traveled to each beachfront community. Yet, the price was prohibitive.

So, I simply considered Farrallon Islands and Half Moon Bay as I might the other side of the moon. It was a concept but nothing reachable or manageable.

July ended and the month I was named after began with me trying to figure out how to overcome the distance between me and Mo. My mom had a car, sort of. It was a Volkswagen Beetle. It was not the new Beetle. It was one of those old Beetles with the battery under the backseat and the engine in the rear, where the trunk should be. My mom loved that car. She had owned it for nearly a decade and if she had her wishes would have it another ten.

That was the extent of my summer. I didn't do much usually, but that summer was particularly boring. My freshman summer ended as uneventful as it had begun. Well, I did have the bare bones of a plan by the beginning of school.

"Auggie, we have to get you your school supplies," my mom announced and the next day we went shopping.

The night before I checked my freshmen school supplies. My backpack had a huge hole in it. I couldn't recall how long the hole had been there. I looked over my polo shirts and khaki pants. I had three gray polo shirts. I had one long-sleeve collared shirt. I had three pair of khaki pants. One pair of pants had a hole in the knee. I needed to get the hole patched.

The next day, while we were shopping, I got new pens, pencils, notebooks and highlighters. My mom had to remind me to look at the school supply list sent by Gee Dub. I needed loose-leaf paper and three binders or a binder keeper that had at least four sections for classes. I decided I needed a new backpack. The khaki pants I had were fine. My mom despite my protest bought me two more pair of pants and three polo shirts. She also got me another long-sleeved white shirt, just in case. The thing which surprised me the most was the Fast Pass my mom bought me. With the Fast Pass I could ride on any bus in the city as long as I had my Fast Pass.

BB was preparing for his freshman year in college. He couldn't give me a ride. He was all the way in Kansas. When school restarted, I found myself on the bus.

The last week of August I woke up at the crack of dawn, washed up, brushed my teeth, dressed and ate breakfast while my mom slept. I could have asked her to drive me to school but it seemed an inconvenience. Instead, I left the house at fifteen minutes to seven and caught the first of two buses to my school.

The first bus, at that hour, was pretty empty. The bus climbed MacArthur Boulevard and chugged along at a snail's pace stopping maybe a dozen times before my stop. I climbed off at High Street and walked two blocks to my second bus stop. At the bus stop were a few faces I recognized from the year before in the halls. I nodded and when the bus arrived climbed on and sat in the back of the bus.

The second bus was a little more crowded, but it was now bustling with Gee Dub students. I sat with my headphones on and rode up the slight hill which led to the switchbacks and finally stopped at the train tracks before making a sharp left turn and letting all of us off to walk the three blocks to Gee Dub.

I fell in line behind some kids I barely knew and trudged past the driveway and to the stone staircase on the side of the hill which belonged to the school.

"Hey, Auggie," Jonathan Garrett chirped as he climbed the stairs two at a time. Jonathan was a bit of a muscle head. He was into extreme sports. I liked him in that I did not hate him.

Jonathan appeared and disappeared in the stream of kids climbing the stairs as I finally reached the parking lot. The climb up the stairs was a good workout. I resigned myself to life on the bus in the morning and after school.

Each day I would get my workout in, climbing the stairs. When school ended, I could head to the bus. I didn't have BB to wait for. I didn't have a reason to stay after school anymore.

I stood in line and gathered my schedule and ID badge and noticed a few new things on my schedule. My advisory teacher was now Mister Pope. BB had given me the scoop on the teacher. Mister Johnson had also suggested Mister Pope might be helpful with Mo.

My advisory was the first period of the day and at the end of the hallway, in the rear of school. I had Math second period, then History and then Spanish before lunch. After lunch I had English, followed by PE and ending my day with Science and Art. The schedule wasn't the best, but it wasn't the worst either.

I was thinking about all sorts of things as I walked down the hall and passed my own Haters Club of Jesse, Del and Percy. Jesse flipped me off. Del sneered. Percy just shook his head as I passed.

Near the library, I ran into Lew, Dre and Rome. We all hugged, dapped and exchanged greetings.

"Where's Will?"

"You didn't hear?"

"No," I said. "What?"

"Will got caught up with some D-boys over the summer," Rome said, with a shake of his head.

"What?"

Rome relayed the story of Will trying his hand at dealing. He wasn't really dealing, according to Rome. He was more a lookout.

"Entry work," Lew said.

"He nearly got a-a-arrested," Dre said, taking a deep breath.

"Is he okay," I asked.

"Not too sure," Rome said. "He is making fast money right now and trying to live like he Billy Bad Ass."

"Is he coming back to school?"

All three looked at me dumbly. Dre shrugged his shoulders. Lew shook his head. Rome lowered his eyes in response.

I nodded. I didn't have anything to say. I felt a little guilty. If Will had found it within himself to trust me, maybe things would have ended differently.

"What you guys thinking?"

"I don't know, maybe, we do one of those interventions," Lew smiled.

"You mean we all go and talk to him?"

"Yeah, that might work," Dre said with a smile.

I nodded. "Okay, count me in. Whatever you guys think. I'm with it."

The first bell rang, and students scrambled, heading to their first period classes.

At room 126 I lined up behind about five other students I knew. At the front was Gregory Bass. He was an overachiever. I knew. Overachievers can tell other overachievers. Behind Bass was Franklin Purcell, a short and fat apple cheeked kid that looked like a black gnome minus the long beard. Behind Purcell was Yvette Denning. Yvette Denning was a dark-skinned girl with a pear shape. She liked to keep her hair in two pigtails on either side of her oval head. In front of me, stood Randy Walsh. He was a tall sophomore who had really long arms and legs. He seemed to be growing into his body.

I looked behind me and came face-to-face with Coke bottle, lower lip biting Terry. She was this wheat-colored beauty with those big brown eyes and full lips.

"Hey," I grunted and tried to play off Terry being so close.

Terry looked at me and nodded.

I was tongue-tied. This was the closest I had been to the bottom lip biter. She smelled liked lavender or honeysuckles. I was wracking my brain for words when out of the corner of my eye a man came fast walking toward the classroom.

The man, a white man, rushed past the line. He was dressed in dark blue trousers, light blue collared shirt and dark blue silk tie. He had short blonde hair, a square jaw and ice blue eyes.

Mister Pope's advisory was unlike any other class I had my sophomore year. It was a class that was very regimented. We had assigned seats. We were expected to use advisory as a study hall if there was nothing assigned to us by Mister Pope, but the best part of advisory was the one-on-one conferences. Once a week Mister Pope had a conference with us, individually. I was scheduled to see him eighteen times a semester, if needed. At the minimum students met with Mister Pope nine times a semester. For the entire year, I calculated, I would sit across the table from Mister Pope nearly forty times.

"Okay, let me clear up some misconceptions right off the bat, this is a graded class. As it is graded, I have to record grades for all of you," Mister Pope explained the first day of school. He was wearing a superhero tie for some reason and I could not help but smile at the idea of a teacher wearing that kind of tie. Pope walked to his desk and grabbed a stack of papers and handed them to the students sitting in the front of the class. He gestured to the students to pass the papers back.

"Advisory is all about helping you succeed at Gee Dub. Everyone will tell you different things about advisory, but it can be the class that helps boost you over the obstacles this year," Mister Pope said as the students passed back the syllabus for the class.

"Because I have to grade you, I have to maintain a record of your work. That's pretty simple. We see each other five times a week. Each day I see you I expect you to write me a paragraph about your day. What you write is for my eyes only, unless you decide to talk about suicide, drug use, harming yourself, harming others or make any mention of use of weapons. I'm your advisory teacher. I'm not a psychologist. All I want to know is that if you are having some issues you have an adult on campus you can talk to."

All the students, including me, were listening. No one said anything.

Mister Pope turned around and pulled up a screen which had been covering his whiteboard. On it were three writing prompts. The first read: "What I hope to do better this year is...."

The second read: "One thing I liked about summer was...." The last read: "One thing you should know about me...."

"Okay, this is your first grade. One paragraph. Not trying to be Hemingway or Chaucer or Baldwin or Richard Wright. Just write."

All the students unzipped their backpacks and gathered their materials. Some asked for pencil and paper.

"Make sure you have your full name on your paper for credit. No name. No credit."

I chose the last writing prompt. I wrote feverishly, as if I had all these ideas locked inside. I had filled the page and flipped it over when I heard Mister Pope speak again.

"Kenya, will you stamp everyone's paper that has at least three sentences. If you don't have three, ask Kenya to come back. You have about seven minutes before we dismiss."

Kenya was a cinnamon brown skinned girl with short hair, apple cheeks, big, full lips and braces. She was a thickly built girl who looked like she was a miniature woman. She stopped at my shoulder and scanned my paper.

"Damn, Auggie, you writing a book," Kenya said with a surprised tone. I looked up and into her deep brown eyes and shook my head.

"Just stamp it."

Kenya in response slammed the stamp in the middle of my paper about three inches from my last word. She grinned and walked away. I watched her retreat and thought for a moment to climb out of my desk and grab the stamp from the little witch and stamp her on her forehead.

Kenya broke my rhythm. So, I looked down on my paper and smiled at the stamp looking back at me. The stamp was of a target with an arrow sticking out of it. At the top it said: You hit the target! I looked at my paper and back at Kenya who was returning the stamp to Mister Pope. I shook my head at Kenya as she sat down. In response Kenya rolled her eyes and started packing up to leave.

With three minutes until the bell Mister Pope spoke again.

"Tommy can you and Pam collect the papers. Tommy you take this half of the class," Mister Pope said with a hand gesture. "Pam you get the other side."

Tommy Livingston was a tall and muscular pecan-colored boy with big ears and the beginnings of a mustache. He had a flat nose above his always puckered lips, big chest and thick arms which had come from years of lifting weights. He was a good athlete and played football, basketball and baseball. I liked Tommy. He was not arrogant like so many high school athletes.

"What up Auggie," Tommy said as I handed him my paper. I nodded. He smiled and showed off his braces.

"Okay, the bell is about to ring but remember I dismiss class not the bell. Remember have something to do or I will find something for you to do in class."

The bell rang. Everyone tensed. Mister Pope smiled.

"You're dismissed."

Students climbed out of their desks and headed for the exit.

After advisory Lew met me and told me to meet him at lunch. He was on his way to History class and heard the teacher was a hardcase.

At lunch we found our new table at the rear of the sophomore tables, but ahead of the freshmen, where we had been the year before.

The crew came up with a plan. It involved Lew's mom dropping us off at Will's house. Lew texted his mom during lunch. Before lunch was over Lew got a text back from his mom. She would drop us off and Lew would have to walk home.

"Okay, we are going to go-go-go and talk to Will," Dre beamed.

"We're all going?"

"Of course, we're all going. He's all of our friend, Lew," Rome said.

It was settled. We all climbed in Missus Holland's car and she drove us back toward my house. Lew sat next to his mom. Dre, Rome and I sat in the backseat and plotted.

"So, what are we going to say?"

"I don't know," said Dre.

"This ends one of two ways," Rome whispered. "Will comes to his senses and realizes that he's throwing away his life. Or he decides that sticking to the straight and narrow is a sap move and tells us to kick rocks."

I listened and nodded. Dre nodded as well.

When Lew's mom dropped us off, I was maybe ten blocks from home. Will lived in the Twenties, or the Twomps, and if you didn't live there you didn't really visit. Lew told his mom that he would walk home after hanging with us. She drove off and left us on the border of the Twomps.

"Okay, where do you think he is," asked Lew.

"Well, wherever they are slinging it, I suppose," said Rome.

I shook my head.

Dre looked around nervously. "I think we should head toward his house. We might run in-in-into him on the way."

That first day, after school, we walked around the Twomps looking for Will. We would have had better luck finding hidden treasure. Lew suggested we walk toward Broadway. Dre suggested we head to Foothill Boulevard. Rome got annoyed and forced us down to East Fourteenth. I didn't have a clue as to where Will might be, so I simply followed.

We walked down to East Fourteenth and then down to Foothill Boulevard. No Will. There were a lot of streetwalkers. There were a few crack heads, but no Will.

"Maybe, one of us can ask one of these fine people where the D-boys are hanging out," Lew suggested as we walked further and further away from Broadway.

"What is your solution," Rome growled, annoyed.

"Okay, we know he lives on two-three, right," I said. I looked around and tried to think. "He ain't watching nothing near his home. He ain't that stupid."

"Yeah," Dre agreed.

"Where are D-boys usually hanging?"

Everyone looked at me as if I had the answer.

"That was a question."

They shook their heads, unsure.

"Well, let's go to the closest liquor store. He might not be there," I said, raising my hands. "But if he ain't he might be closer than on some main drag like this."

"Yeah," Dre agreed.

We were close to Foothill and on the corner of Foothill and East Fourteenth was a corner liquor store. Across the street on the other corner was a shoe store. On the other corner of the intersection was one of those markets that passed as a clothing store, swap meet or whatever. On the corner on the side where the liquor store was sat a Wendy's.

"Look," said Dre, pointing toward the Wendy's.

We all looked and there was Will with two other boys who looked like they were fresh out of high school or lock up.

"Oh, snap," said Lew. He put a hand to his mouth as if he had seen a gruesome accident. Lew slowed.

Rome and Dre reached out and pushed Lew forward.

"What did you think this was going to be some made for TV moment?"

"Hell, I have to say I don't know what I expected, but I definitely didn't think he would be with some thuggies."

"Squash that," I said. Will was our friend. He was my oldest friend. We had our ups and downs, but at the end we were still friends. Nothing broke that up.

"Come on," I said and ran across the four lanes of traffic to Will and the two strangers. Lew paused. Dre and Rome followed behind me. Lew walked to the corner and stood at the light waiting for the traffic to stop.

Will seeing us looked at his friends and said something and they nodded and walked toward the rear of Wendy's.

Will turned and looked at us like we were crazy.

Will nodded and smiled, but he seemed guarded for some reason. He was dressed to show off the waistband of his gym shorts, baggy jeans, a thick leather belt, a tank top T-shirt, and some Timberlands. Behind his ear was a Cigarillo. He sneered at us, the corner of his right lip snarling just enough to show a few clenched teeth.

"What up, Will," Rome said, awkwardly. He stopped short noticing Will was not smiling but watching him.

Dre stopped and I studied Will not sure how to proceed.

"What are you doing man," I asked, deciding the only tact was the one where we cut through the politeness and dealt with the real problem.

"What you talking about Auggie," Will smiled, turning to me and for the first time I noticed his eyes were a little glazed.

"You give up on school?"

Will smiled, snarled. He looked at me like I was a thing and not someone who had known him for years. I wanted to snatch Will from the fast-food restaurant and beat some sense into him. I was thinking of that when a dark blue 300 slid up and honked the horn. One of the nameless strangers rolled down the window and said, "Dub, we got to go."

"You keep that stuff for you and your fam," Will said, looking at the dark blue 300 and taking a couple of steps in the direction of the car. "I got to make decisions for me."

With that Will bounced to the 300 and climbed into the back and the car slipped into traffic and in minutes was gone. Lew walked up as I watched the dark blue 300 drive away and disappear in the sea of cars on East Fourteenth.

"What happened?"

I shook my head. I spun on my heels. I decided to walk up Foothill back toward my home. The three talked but I didn't have anything to say.

"You think he's coming back?"

"We can always hope, but I ain't going to hold my breath," Rome said.

"He's caught up now," Dre said.

"Yeah," Lew agreed. "Those guys he was with did not look cool at all."

"What should we do?"

"What do you mean?"

"I mean, that's Will, he's our friend and he's screwed up," I said angry with myself. "He's caught up with the wrong crowd. You know how this ends. He climbs to the top and someone knocks him off or he crosses someone, and they murk him."

"Or he ju-ju-just gets smoked in some ran-ran-random shooting," Dre said. He shook his head.

"Should we go to his mom?"

I shook my head. I was the only one Will ever told the truth about the person raising him. She wasn't his biological mother. She was his aunt. His mother's sister was raising him and at times Will pushed her. She was always threatening to kick him out. She wouldn't shed a tear hearing Will had decided to become independent. He was one less mouth to feed.

"We are Will's family," I said. "If he's on the street then we have to get him back."

Lew and Rome turned on Twentieth and headed south, parallel to my home. Dre lived four blocks from me. So, he and I walked to the 7-11 before saying goodbye.

"What you thinking?"

"I think we need to find him and try and talk some sense into him until he tells us to kick rocks. Until then, there's a chance," I said.

Dre nodded. We fist bumped, hugged and walked in opposite directions. I headed home thinking about Will and what I could say to convince someone caught up on the streets to give it up and return to school.

That night my mom noticed my change of behavior. I was quieter than usual. I quickly had a lot on my mind. Since seeing Will and walking home I had been wrestling with the seemingly unsolvable problem of convincing Will to give up the street and return to school.

"You okay, baby?"

"No, not really," I admitted.

"What's going on," my mom asked as she sat and had dinner. My mom had made a salad, some mashed potatoes, corn on the cob and fried chicken. I was drinking some tropical punch. My mom was drinking green tea.

I hemmed and hawed. I didn't need to burden my mom with something I was trying to figure out. I couldn't imagine my mom had ever had a situation like I was wrestling with.

"I'm just trying to try and motivate a friend in school," I finally said.

My mom listened. She gave me a couple of pieces of chicken and scooped two big heaps of mash potatoes on my plate. I grabbed an ear of corn and forked out some salad.

"Well, I have always believed that you can't motivate someone else," my mom said with her buttery singsong voice. I loved listening to her talk. As she spoke, I looked at her high cheekbones and slightly round nose. Like my mom, I knew I had the sprinkle of freckles on my cheeks and the bridge of my nose from some slaveowner and rapist back in our lineage.

"The closest you can get is giving them the options and letting them decide. You are only responsible for you, Auggie. You can't be worrying about everybody else no matter how much you care."

I listened. I knew my mom meant well. I just didn't think she understood the situation.

Chapter 12.

September through December

School, because of Will, started slowly and I didn't feel like I got going, mentally until the end of the first six weeks. Will and the street troubled me. I felt like I was walking in mud every day I was at Gee Dub. When there were moments, and there were too many moments, I found myself thinking about what Will was doing? Was he on the streets? Had he moved out of his aunt's apartment? Where was he staying? My mind just ricocheted from scenario to scenario and each street drama ended with Will standing with someone holding a gun on him.

From the end of August to the middle of November Dre, Lew, Rome or I went to the Twomps to convince Will school was the only real option. Dre came back heart broken. Lew didn't want to go back. Rome said that Will and he had a good conversation. Of course, no one believed Rome. Will hated Rome.

My last November talk with Will was more an argument than an attempt to convince. I couldn't help it. The new Will annoyed me. He was so smug and sure of himself.

I had found him where Rome told me he had talked to Will. I saw him as I walked up the street toward him. He was leaning against an abandoned building in the middle of the street. As I got close, I noticed Will had a scar on his cheek that looked like a knife had left the thin scar.

"Will, you are being selfish," I began, the anger rising in my voice like the bile in my stomach seeing my friend dressed in Timberlands, the elastic waistband of his gym shorts visible above his baggy jeans, a cartoon T-shirt and a puff coat. We were on a street which had a liquor store on the corner and at the other end a main street.

"What you're doing is killing everyone that loves and cares about you."

"Ain't nobody that loves me," the transformed Will snarled.

"What about Dre? Or Rome? Or Lew?"

"Y'all a bunch of squares and feel guilty. Tell them they didn't do nothing. This was my choice," Will smirked.

"We ain't coming down here for our own good," I spat. "You selfish hardheaded punk, you got us all twisted about you and this," I waved around him. We were just four blocks away from his aunt's apartment, but it could have been four light years as I talked. "This ain't a life, Will. You know that. In the end, this ends with you as a chalk outline."

"Auggie, you don't know what you're talking about. This ain't no movie. This ain't no book," Will looked around him as he leaned against the front of the boarded-up building, he was posted at that moment. "This is real. It is as real as it gets." He paused. "You know all the books you going to read ain't ever going to prepare you for the grab and take world we live in."

"That ain't no life," I repeated.

"You go back to that school and let them train you to accept the scraps they brushing off the table," Will frowned. He shook his head.

"What? You talking craziness."

"Craziness? Think that this system is all screwed up for you and me. We ain't given a fair chance from the moment we take our first breath." Will shook his head. "You been brainwashed, and I just figured things ain't ever going to be better than they are now."

"Will, you need to come back to school," I said, frustrated.

"You don't get it. The few nights and days I have been out here has taught me more than all the years of school before," Will said, his dark eyes thin and serious. "You go. Tell the others to stop coming. I don't want to talk to them no more. There ain't no way for me to come back. I'm done. Tell them that. I'm done."

I had no words. I looked at Will and didn't recognize him anymore. I turned and walked away from the person I had known since second grade.

Two weeks before Thanksgiving break students decorated the hallways with Thanksgiving inspired things. Gee Dub, during the holidays, was an amazing place. In just a few days Gee Dub was transformed. There were fall leaves cut out and pasted everywhere. In each hall there was a distinct and unique theme. I loved the Native American hallway which Mister Troy supervised.

To cap off the hard work done by students there was a Thanksgiving assembly. At the assembly there was dancing, singing and a step show.

The highlight of the Thanksgiving assembly was the teacher performance. A group of teachers would get on stage and perform for the students. The assembly the eve of Thanksgiving had four teachers shine. There was Mister Ross, Missus Bluford, Missus Collins and Mister Pope. The four were school favorites.

Mister Ross was this gap-toothed walnut block of a man and an amateur magician. Mister Ross, my science teacher, did a short sleight of hand show magic show for the crowd. He invited several students onstage and dazzled and amazed everyone in the crowd pulling scarves out of student's ears. The showstopper was finding a lost card. Mister Ross was a great magician and teacher.

Missus Collins was one of the PE teachers and had been a drum majorette at her college. She slipped on her college drum majorette outfit from her HBCU, including the tall hat and baton, and did a short cheer from her college for everyone.

Missus Bluford's talent was juggling. She was the cheerleading coach. Missus Bluford did a dangerous juggling act that included bowling pins and machetes. She was joined onstage by her dance team and a group of cheerleaders. The dance team and cheerleaders danced along with Missus Bluford to the screams and cheers from everyone.

Mister Pope, in college, had been a part of the college choir and loved to sing. He sang a song everyone knew from the radio. My favorite memory of Mister Pope was him onstage singing three Christmas favorites and mixing them into a funky and enjoyable medley. The songs were Twelve Days of Christmas, Frosty the

Snowman and Rudolph the Red Nose Reindeer. Mister Pope had a good voice and the chops to sing. He was surprisingly talented and could break up the classics so everyone in the assembly sang a portion of the song in rounds. It was a great moment. I liked that Mister Pope did not take himself too seriously. To me, that was a good characteristic in a teacher.

Maybe a week before Thanksgiving break, I sat in the lunchroom and relayed the conversation I had with Will.

"What does that mean?"

"What do you think it means?"

"We giving up?"

"I don't know," I said. "My mom told me you can't motivate others."

We didn't decide then and there. It was more like a slow tearing off a Band-Aid. We knew we had to tear it off, but we balked. Rome was the first to say the words everyone was thinking.

"I can't make Will do anything. We can't make him do anything even if we pray and go down there every day. He made his decision. He knows what's out there."

"So," Dre said.

"So, we let him go."

"Like that?"

Lew agreed. Dre agreed. Eventually, even I agreed.

After we returned from Thanksgiving break, we all agreed on letting Will go his way. The decision wasn't easy, even for Rome who had a fractured relation with Will. It was not like we could turn off our feelings, but we tried.

At the lunch table BB was a brief topic, but Will dropping out haunted us all.

"Man, we have to move on," Rome said. "We all ain't made the same."

"Jus-just- just hard," Dre stammered.

"Hell, we all tried."

"We can't jump in the hole with Will and lift him out," I said. I was annoyed. "We have a better chance of helping him if we succeed and then go back and get him."

We focused on other things. I put my attention elsewhere. There were several other things to concentrate on in Gee Dub. Before Will derailed I had planned a way to get us all into college. So, I refocused and concentrated on that rough idea of a plan.

Before Christmas break, I decided to launch the idea which had been rattling around in my head for some time. Sitting at home Thanksgiving I sort of sketched out a plan. Seeing it on paper always made it seem more believable.

"Okay, we have just a couple of weeks before the first half of the school year is over. I know we have talked about this before, but I think I have a plan for all of us to succeed," I said.

We were at our sophomore table with maybe a dozen other people in the lunchroom.

"The way I see it, everyone wants to go to college. Right?"

No one disagreed.

"Well, I was reading this magazine during my freshman exile," I said.

"Your self-imposed exile for being stupid," Rome said with a smile.

"Anyway, while I was alone, I found there was all this information," I said. I pulled the magazine from my backpack. Lew was the first to snatch it from me. He looked at it and passed it to Dre. Dre tried to look at it and listen but handed it to Rome. Rome leafed through the magazine and listened.

"There are a million ways to get to college, Auggie," Rome smirked. "But getting into college ain't possible for everyone."

"But it is if we can overcome the cost and the application," I smiled at Rome.

"Auggie, we've all heard this speech from the counselors," Lew said.

"Yeah," I said, with a nod. "But the difference is that I have a plan for all of us to go to college and the college of our choice."

"What kind of plan?"

"It's a two-prong plan," I began. "I was reading about scholarships. College is expensive. The biggest hurdle to going to college is it is usually too expensive."

"Again, Auggie, we all know this," Lew smirked. "Come to think of it I think there are at least three of us who will be trying to get over that hurdle."

I shook my head. I refused to be derailed. I continued. "So, I have a list of scholarships I will give to all of you. According to the magazine there was this girl Valerie Cooper who came up, mostly, on the smaller thousand- and ten-thousand-dollar scholarships and avoiding the bigger scholarships."

"What?"

"She avoided those super competitive scholarships and got over $100k in scholarships," I said and waited for everyone to react.

They didn't react. I suppose that was a reaction.

"So, she began this around the same time as us," I continued.

"Why," asked Lew.

"I think she needed time," I admitted. "It takes time to fill out and find the right scholarships."

"It seems that the smart move is to apply for the bigger scholarships," Rome pointed out.

"The way I see it the bigger the scholarship the more the competition," I explained. "You know how many of us have won the Bill Gates Millenium Scholarship?"

No one answered.

"None. That's right all the biggest brains in the nation apply for that one scholarship," I said.

"Seriously?"

"I bet the first one who does win will go to some private college prep or academy," Lew said.

"I might a-a-apply for that scho-scho-scholarship," said Dre annoyed.

"That doesn't matter. All that matters is we all get some scholarships," I said, a little annoyed.

"Where's the list?"

I handed out the copies. They flipped through the papers. Dre and Lew were bored.

"Hey, that scholarship is on this list," Rome said.

Everyone looked and saw the Millenium Scholarship web address.

"It's there because it's a scholarship that is open to all students. I wasn't going to remove it from the list. All I'm saying is that we should concentrate on scholarships that won't have a million people applying for it." I paused. I focused. "The only thing is that if you find a scholarship that you apply for then you should tell us all."

Rome nodded. Dre listened. Lew studied me earnestly.

"Wait," Dre said. "I thought scholar-scholar-scholarships were not for-for-for soph-soph-sophomores."

"Well, technically, you are right," I said. "We can apply as long as we're in high school and bank the money," I giggled. "I asked the counselor."

"It's not nice to laugh at people," Lew said with a smile.

I ignored Lew and soldiered on. "That's the first part. I suggest that we begin applying now. My personal goal is to apply for at least fifty scholarships." I paused. "The article said that girl applied to over sixty. So, I figure we can write to a bunch of scholarships. The people making decisions want us to get into college. So, we have that going for us."

"How you know that?"

"They don't want college to be snow white," I said. "The world's changed."

The three looked at each other, unsure.

"Sixty?"

"I say anything on the right side of twenty is a good bet," I said to Rome.

"You can do that?"

"There is no limit on scholarship applications," I said to Rome. "Oh, and many scholarships have requirements. So, keep your grades up. And we avoid all those scholarships that asks for money." I stopped and looked at my friends. "I suppose that we could talk to the counselor and see if we can get waivers."

"That's a given," Lew smiled.

"Maybe we set a goal," Dre said.

"We don't have to do too many, but we should do some. The second part is the hardest." I paused. "So, we apply to a bunch of scholarships. That's on us. Then we get our college lists together. Dream schools. Local schools. Out of state schools. Again, that's the easy stuff. Now, the hardest part is trying to figure out a way to separate us from the rest of the thousands and thousands of other applicants trying to get in college."

Lew whistled.

"How we going to separate us from those hundreds of thousands," asked Rome.

"Well, I don't know," I admitted. "Based on the magazine colleges like community service."

Lew shook his head.

"Community service?"

"Well, all colleges want someone that is more than just a grade point average or an athlete," I said. "I mean, not everyone that goes to college plays sports. It's cool to play sports, I guess," I tried. "I don't play sports." I shook my head. "All I am saying is that colleges are looking for, according to the magazine, someone that will improve their college and has an interest in community or worldwide issues."

Rome and Dre looked at each other, confused.

"Wait," Dre said. "What a-a-about the bird that got lost?"

"No, I think that is a no go. There's no way to save that bird. It's impossible," I said, a little annoyed the bird's predicament had stumped me.

"Community interests," Lew said, with a smile. He nodded. "You know how you guys give me grief about caring about the planet?"

"Yeah, yeah," Dre said, rolling his eyes.

"It's not just us," Rome smiled.

"Well, if you want a great project," Lew began.

"Don't tell us about recycling," Rome growled. "I'm not going to spend a year educating people to reduce, reuse and recycle." Rome looked at Lew menacingly. "I ain't."

"My point is that we need to start thinking about our community or the world if we want to go to college."

"Recycling or water pollution is an easy project," Lew said.

Dre rolled his eyes at Lew. Rome shook his head. I smiled.

"I think it should be something that you want to do with or without the scholarship or college," I said.

"Man, Auggie, I don't think everyone that goes to college cares about the community. I know I don't think too much about the world," Rome admitted.

"I bet BB didn't have to talk too-too-too much about com-com-community service," Dre smirked.

"I don't know too many people our age, other than Lew, that are all into that."

"That's my point," I said. "We're trying to distinguish ourselves from everyone else."

The three fell silent.

"So, that's my idea. Scholarships and separating ourselves from the crowd," I said with a smile. "The thing is that if we work together, we are more likely to succeed than by ourselves."

"Yeah," said Rome. Everyone agreed.

The last week of November and Lew and Dre were smiling from ear-to-ear when I sat at the lunch table.

"I applied to my first scholarship," Lew said.

"Me too," Dre said.

Lew and Dre had sent in their first scholarship and were on pins and needles trying to find out when they would know if they got their scholarship. Rome was sulking. He was going to send in three scholarship applications after Christmas break. He had decided to focus on three programs which focused on left-handed, black and urban students.

In English class Mister Sanderson made all the students in class get a headache when he tried to explain existential thinking. The lesson was free willing as he mentioned all these philosophers. The headache came when Mister Sanderson explained that Buddha, the god who came to earth to enlighten others, had suggested that 90% of the people walk around and move and live in a sort of sleeping existence. Mister Sanderson called those people "sleepwalkers." They are always bored. They are never entertained. They have their eyes open, but they do not see anything. They are simply going through the motions. The others, the 10%, are awake, alive and experience the world like no one else. Food tastes better. Every experience is incredible. When you meet those people, you know you are with someone who is living. The very experience is electric. Mister Sanderson asked before the end of the class if students were sleepwalking or awake. It was an interesting question.

December was a short month and a few days before school let out for the year there was a big commotion in the gym. I walked by thinking there might be a fight. Curious, I looked through the people gathered at the closed gym.

There was my cousin, BB sitting in the bleachers with a bunch of people around him. Seeing my cousin made me smile. BB was dressed in a blue Kansas hooded sweatshirt. He was a little thicker, I noticed. He was wearing acid washed jeans and a crisp pair of Nikes. His appearance got everyone talking, like a celebrity was on campus.

I pushed through the crowd and into the gym and found BB sitting with his old coach and about ten other basketball players. Around them were about one hundred students taking pictures and elbowing each other and trying to get BB's attention. There were two security officers watching the door and two camera crews recording.

I snaked my way through the crowd and security and stepped in the inner circle of BB's basketball friends. There were cameras set up and reporters with microphones talking to BB. One of BB's basketball friends put out a hand to stop me from interrupting the interview.

"So, it is nice to find you back at your old stomping grounds for a little while," one of the reporters, a moon-face woman with a thin red mouth smiled, dressed in a suit jacket and jeans.

"Yeah, the coach told me it would be okay to come home and work on my shooting before things started getting serious."

"Benaiah, everyone wants to know," the second reporter, dark-haired man with a half moonish jaw began, speaking into the microphone. "Do you think you will be starting over Edwards this year?"

"Well, you know I am a freshman and there are a lot of seasoned players on the squad. I think that the coach wants to give me some time, early in the season. Based on that we'll see."

The interview wrapped up and the coach and the reporters thanked each other. The interview took about ten minutes from the time I was there.

BB seeing me, stood up and smiled.

"What's up, little man?"

I didn't realize how badly I missed BB until I was close enough to touch him. We hugged. He laughed at my embrace.

"Okay, Auggie," BB said. "I can't be hugged by everybody. I won't have no time to do anything before I have to go back to school."

"How long you here?"

"A few days after Christmas," BB said. "I'm supposed to be at a Christmas tournament, then pre-season and regular season."

"You like it there," I asked.

"It's cool."

I studied BB. He looked good and relaxed.

"You keeping your grades up?"

BB turned to his coach and old teammates and smiled. "See, I told you. I always got Auggie to keep me straight and focused on grades and the like." He turned back to me with a gentle smile. "I'm here for a minute, if you need a ride, I've got the 'stang."

I nodded.

School, after seeing BB, was just a countdown to the end of Art class and catching a ride home with my cousin. When the bell rang, and we were dismissed I headed to the parking lot and there was BB. The Mustang was still beautiful and dangerous looking.

"How you doing?"

I looked at BB. I knew the question wasn't just some politeness. BB was curious about my school year.

"Things are good," I said as the Mustang rumbled to life. "Will dropped out."

"What?"

"Yeah, we tried to get him back, but he's out."

BB listened.

"Streets," I added.

"Call of the streets," BB finally said as we slid out of the parking lot.

I nodded.

"Why you here?"

BB smiled. "I need to train while I'm off campus. Figure that the best place is here."

I nodded. I really didn't care why BB was at school. I was just glad he was there.

For four days it felt like I was a freshman again. BB picked me up in the morning and took me to Gee Dub. He dropped me off and talked with his old teachers. He was working on his skills in the gym from lunch until school let out. The PE teachers loved pointing out BB working out.

I sat in the Mustang and just enjoyed being with BB and let slip I was thinking of going to the Twomps one last time to try and convince Will to come back to school. Immediately, I felt I had said too much. BB didn't say anything. He just drove and let the Mustang purr. On some street we drove down toward my house BB finally spoke.

"You know you can't make me eat okra," BB said as we drove home, after school.

"What?"

"I know that my moms loves it. She loves it. I think my dads likes it too. But its my moms favorite," BB said as he drove slowly in the growling Mustang.

"Okay," I said, not knowing how BB got on the topic of his mom's favorite food.

"She tried to get me to like it." BB smiled. "I just don't like it. It didn't matter what she said or did, and that's my moms."

"So, why you telling me this," I said, feeling my cousin was just trying to fill the silence.

"Think about that the next time you trying to save someone," BB said.

I was the smart one of the pair of us, I wanted to say. I balled my fist and thought about punching BB in the shoulder but thought better of it. I didn't respond. He would have loved me saying something, but I didn't give him that.

Christmas break began and when I got home, I found myself sad. I guess in the quiet the weight of the decision, the group decision, hit me hard. I had known Will since second grade.

We, Rome, Lew, Dre and I, had decided it was for the best to let Will try to survive on the streets. It was beyond awkward. He was our friend, one day, then nobody, the next.

For five days of my break, I thought of going to the Twomps and finding Will and just seeing him. I didn't want to talk to him. I just wanted to make sure he was okay.

I texted Dre, Lew and Rome and watched Netflix in my pajamas. There were full days when I never changed out of my pajamas. My mom laughed at my laziness.

When my mom took me over to BB's house, Lourdes, twelve and full of spit and vinegar, opened the door dressed in her newest Christmas outfit. She was wearing a True Religion hoody, skinny jeans and Uggs. Lourdes tilted her head to the side and showed off her new cell phone. She hugged my mom and looked at me like I was a flea-ridden dog entering her house. Her disgust melted when she saw I was carrying gift wrapped presents.

"Merry Christmas, Auggie," Lourdes said, eyeing the presents.

"Merry Christmas, Lourdes," I said.

"You can put the presents under the tree," Lourdes said as she ushered us into their home.

BB was leaning against the entrance to the living room dressed like he was going out, dressed in distressed jeans. I noted the new basketball sneakers and his fresh, brand new Kansas college hoody.

My mother gave BB a hug and entered the main part of the house. Lourdes hovered. I put the presents under the tree and Lourdes, seeing her present instantly lost interest and drifted back toward the kitchen still on her new phone.

BB smiled as Lourdes pushed past her older brother.

"What you trying to be in the school catalog or something," I asked.

"Thought it was appropriate and all," BB replied.

"BB don't go to college and become all stuck up. I mean, you ain't too far from that now, come to think of it," I laughed.

BB shook his head and walked me into the main area of the house. My uncle and aunt were seated on the couch watching a football game. My mom sat next to her brother and already had a glass of eggnog in her hand. My family loved sports.

We had a great Christmas dinner. My aunt Arna made a deep-fried turkey. There was green beans, mashed potatoes, yams, corn on the cob as well as honey dipped biscuits and cornbread. Lourdes bragged about helping make the cranberry sauce. For dessert, there was pumpkin, apple and a blueberry pie.

After dinner BB and I took a walk. We didn't go too far.

"What's going on BB?"

"Nothing," BB lied. He was a terrible liar.

"Come on, man," I said.

BB looked like he was unsure how to say what was on his mind, and then and there I knew he had something bugging him. I waited him out. I knew he would tell. We walked to the end of the street and turned right and walked another block before BB spoke.

"Remember Latoya?"

I nodded.

"She's pregnant," BB said, his eyes refused to look at me.

I stopped with the news. I wasn't sure what it meant to BB. Almost instantly I had a flood of thoughts in my head.

"What are you going to do?"

BB looked at me. There was this uncertainty in my cousin I had never seen before. I felt I had pushed him too far with the question. I wanted to take back what I said.

BB rubbed the back of his neck, before he spoke. "I'm not even sure it's mine."

I didn't respond.

"I mean, I was away in college. How does she come up pregnant," BB said through gritted teeth. "How she going to claim it's mine, at that?"

I listened.

"I think that I'm done with this place, Auggie," BB said. "Everybody is all in my mix. They want to know what I'm going to do next." He paused. "They ain't got lives? They ain't got things to worry about?" He looked at me angry. He shook his head.

I stood on the corner and listened to BB. I could tell he was upset. I recalled before Thanksgiving there were rumors about Latoya, but I never bit. I just listened.

"I just want to go to college and play basketball," BB said. "Now, I mean, everyone here is so small time. They ain't dreaming. They are just stealing people's dreams."

BB and I stood on the corner for a few moments. I didn't dare offer my thoughts. I mean, I was just a sophomore and just happy to have my friends.

BB spun on his heels and began walking back down the street. I followed.

"You guard your dreams," BB said as we turned left on his street. "Don't let people steal your dreams. You have to fight for what you're dreaming about."

I did not disagree. There was nothing to say. I just walked with my cousin and let him have his quiet.

The next day we drove BB to the airport, and he flew to Hawaii to meet with his college team for a Christmas basketball tournament. The perks of being on a championship college basketball team.

Chapter 13.

After Christmas break, we focused on scholarships. Rome had sent in his three applications. Lew and Dre were trying to decide when to contact the scholarship people to make sure they received their applications.

School restarted in January. Everyone for a few days wished everyone a happy New Year. I thought the wishes were a great unifying thing. For a few days I had other things on my mind.

I tried to not get all caught up in when I would hear from my first scholarship. I just studied the list and tried to think what scholarship I would apply for that month. I went to class. I saw Mercedes in Math and Science and heard through the high school grapevine she and Franco were over. She was single for the moment.

"You know she's going to be hooked up with someone soon," Grace Patterson, one of the girls in our Math class said to someone in earshot.

Franco was now dating a junior named Nicole. I listened to the gossip but was not interested any longer in Mercedes Copeland. I had other things to worry about.

BB texted me three words one day in January and for the entire day I could not stop smiling. I know he was happy. I was happy too for BB. The message read: "It's not mine."

The first month of the new school year ended and I was trying to wrap my head around the idea of a community or world issue and what determined the difference. The problem about the concept was a community issue could be a world issue. My question was, could a world issue be a community issue?

In the back of my mind, I was leaning toward devoting all my energy to saving someone who didn't want to be saved. It was not a world issue, but it was a community issue, I was convinced.

A few days later, I found myself thinking about a way to save someone who didn't want to be saved and taking the concept to the crew when the lost bird topic reared its head again.

In advisory Mister Pope was this fount of knowledge in a sea of instructors. The thing I liked most about Mister Pope was he never talked down to any of us. I knew he was smart, but he never held his degree or where he went to college over us. I liked that he didn't back down from anyone. He was tough but also cared.

My first few conferences with Mister Pope were incredible. I had watched the conferences from afar so was not surprised when my chance to sit with my advisory teacher came up. He called me to his desk and went through my entire schedule and my grades. The first conferences he gave general advice. Each meeting Mister Pope seemed to be current on my academic progress.

"August, you are an aspiring George Washington Carver scholar," Mister Pope said admiring my blue blazer and the scholar lapel pin from his desk. I listened and studied the man talking and the various things on his desk. There were paperclipped piles of papers stacked neatly on the far end of his desk. His desk was cluttered with various things. I noted his hand sanitizer. There was also a coffee cup which read: "Need More Coffee." Behind Pope were two calendars attached to the wall. One calendar was the district calendar which was three times its normal size. The other calendar, which looked like the district calendar, had names penciled in Monday through Friday. There were no more than three names each day. Quick math meant of the twenty-five students in advisory he saw fifteen a week. Every marking period he scheduled a meeting with everyone. Of course, not everyone needed a weekly meeting. At the minimum, in thirty-six weeks of school I would see Mister Pope at least eighteen times.

"Your grades are top notch. I suppose you know that already." Mister Pope paused and looked at me with those ice blue eyes. He was a tan man maybe forty but in shape, not forty and pudgy. "What do you want to learn in advisory class to make you a better person?"

I was confused. I didn't know what I wanted to do to be a better person. The question seemed bigger than what I expected.

"I don't expect you to know exactly, but I want you to think about what it would take for you to be a better person." Mister Pope paused and looked at me. "August, you have any questions?"

I shook my head. Mister Pope nodded. I climbed up from my seat after the first of four conferences with Mister Pope.

"Do me a favor and tell Heaven that I need to see her?"

I nodded and headed to my seat. I tapped Heaven and pointed to Mister Pope. The boyish Heaven Ashland with her small eyes, wide mouth and long legs climbed to her feet. I sat and tried to think about what Mister Pope asked. I wondered if he asked everyone the same question?

I leaned over to James Price, a thin brown boy with a tight fade and a zig zag part cut into the side of his peanut shaped head. He had an overbite and a peach fuzz mustache above his full lips. He was a long, spidery kid who looked like he might be mixed with peanuts, aliens or spidery black people. James was an okay character but not someone I talked to outside of advisory class.

When I leaned over, James was curled around his writing trying to compose his daily writing.

"James," I said. "What did Pope ask you when you talked to him?"

James looked up with his big eyes, curious and annoyed.

"You talked with him yesterday. Right?"

"Yeah."

"What did he ask you?"

James did not respond to the question immediately. He just looked at me for a long moment with his big eyes, overbite and spidery fingers holding his pencil in his thin hand.

"What do you mean," James said in a slow and deliberate fashion.

"When you had your conference with Pope," I began slowly, trying not to sound annoyed, but annoyed. "Did he ask you anything?"

"Yeah, he wanted to know how come I wasn't turning in my Math homework. He had my grades in front of him. He asked about the three classes I was not doing well in. I think he offered to tutor me or get a tutor for me." James paused, thinking. "I think that was all." He looked at me and smiled. "Why you asking?"

"I just was curious."

"You suppose to be my tutor?"

"No," I said with a shake of my head. "Thanks," I said and turned and shuffled some papers and pretended to be busy.

"I heard that you were good with writing," the boy with the peach fuzz mustache said.

"I'm okay," I said. "What you need help with?"

James smiled. "I just never know how to start the writing. I'm trying to knock out the daily paragraph thing for advisory."

I nodded. I looked at James' empty page and smiled.

"Well, I like to think of things like math," I began. "Numbers are easy and simple. Zero to ten easy. For me, I learned that writing is all about numbers too."

"What?"

"Just listen," I said. "How many sentences in a paragraph?"

James looked at me silently, thinking.

I smiled and didn't want him to feel too uncomfortable.

"Five sentences. So, when I write I think that I have to write five sentences. That's it. If I have to write a page that might be fifteen sentences or three paragraphs." I paused. I let what I said sink in. "It's math."

"Okay, but how do I begin?"

"There are tons of ways to start. You can ask a question. You can use a quote. You can make a joke. There are too many ways to begin." I paused. I saw James looking at me with a blank stare. "I usually ask a question or use a quote. We all know quotes. We hear them all the time." I paused. I could see James needed a little push. "So, this is advisory. I would start out with something funny or silly. Like, "Too often I ask for advice. In advisory, though, I don't have to ask. The whole class is about advising me.""

"I like that," James nodded. He looked at me and then at his paper and began to write.

"That's my suggestion," I said and turned away. I looked at my notebook and opened it and checked the time. Advisory class was only thirty minutes. I found a blank page in the notebook and started to doodle. I looked back and James was trying to write his paragraph.

I almost laughed out loud when I heard him repeating what I had said, as he wrote.

School was like an echo chamber. Someone would say something and someone else would say something and then everyone would believe it. High school.

It was a good and bad thing. Gee Dub had fights now and then based on something someone said. The rumor mill was vicious. I tried to avoid it with all the power in me. When BB was around my first year, I was insulated from it. With my star basketball cousin gone I was suddenly vulnerable.

The last week of January, I had my tenth conference with Mister Pope.

"August, did you think about what you want to learn to be a better person?"

I was stunned, honestly. I didn't think Mister Pope would remember let alone ask me something we had discussed nearly three weeks ago, but he did.

"Well, come to think of it," I smiled, impressed with Mister Pope for all sorts of reasons. "I have been thinking about ways to be a better person in the future. I would like to understand how going to college actually matters. I don't mean, why college? I mean what is the benefit of college?"

Mister Pope nodded. He pursed his thin lips. It looked like Mister Pope was deep in thought.

"Well, college isn't for everybody, if I'm being honest. I mean, there are some really successful people who didn't go to college. But those same people had other forms of help." Pope paused, thinking. "I think someone like you needs to go to college to see what is possible. What you learn here is just practice. In college you get to see all types of possibilities. High school is just like network TV. There's only those ten or twenty channels available. College is cable or satellite TV. You have hundreds of choices."

I listened and nodded.

"So, I go to college I get a job, then what?"

"There's no guarantees in this world, August. When I was in college the teachers always told us about all the students with Ph.Ds. who decided to be garbagemen."

"What you mean? I could go to college and not get a job?"

Pope nodded.

I let the words and idea sink in.

"The difference is going to college gives you the opportunity to work wherever you fill you are qualified. There are going to be obstacles everywhere. But with a college diploma you can get into the doors that are closed to those without a high school diploma or only a high school diploma."

I nodded.

"You've asked some great questions."

I pivoted. "Mister Pope, if I decide to go to college, I have noticed there is a part of the application that asks about community service. Can you tell me what that means?"

"I know you are kidding, but community service can be anything that you do for your community," Mister Pope said with a slight smile.

"No, I know what community service is by definition," I said looking past Mister Pope to the calendar behind him. Based on the calendar we only had two school days before the three-day Martin Luther King Jr. break. "I was curious what colleges are looking for when they say community service? I mean, I think I get the general idea, on the high school level, but I doubt that the admission department would be blown away by a recycling program or reading to elementary kids." I paused. "I want to know what community service the colleges are looking for that would separate me from other applicants."

Mister Pope nodded. He pressed his thin lips together for a moment, thinking. He closed his eyes for a moment before speaking.

"The way I see it," Mister Pope began with a wry smile. "Colleges want students that have a real love for something that matters to them and their community. They don't want something that is temporary or only done to pad the application or on the spur of the moment. Colleges are looking for a well-rounded individual," Mister Pope concluded.

"Thanks," I said and climbed to my feet. I was flummoxed. I had no idea of what community project would be something my friends and I could embrace that would not be seen as padding or filler and we all would want to participate in without coercion. I sat in my seat and wracked my brain about projects around the community.

During the first three-day break of the new year Rome texted me and told me to meet him outside in five minutes.

I walked outside and found Rome and Dre standing on the opposite side of the street, in front of a huge silver Lincoln Navigator.

As soon as I saw the two amigos I smiled. I was looking for Lew. It was surprising not to see the tree-hugger with Dre or Rome.

"This you?"

"Pops came up," Rome beamed.

"But, how?"

"My dad made me take some classes with someone he hired," Rome said with a shake of his head. He quickly displayed his license.

Auggie just shook his head.

"Rome got a Navi," Dre crowed.

"A Navi," I repeated.

"Man, how did that happen?"

"I don't really know, honestly," Rome said. He was wearing a new outfit. He had a new pair of kicks on, new jeans and a True Religion hooded sweatshirt. On his wrist was a G-Shock.

Dre shook his head. He looked at me and smiled and I knew the SUV was not a no strings attached kind of gift. "Get in, we'll drive around and test out the Navi."

I walked around the front of the silver SUV's chrome front grill and noticed Lew seated in the passenger seat. I shook my head.

Climbing into the second row of seats next to Dre and I laughed at Lew. I looked back and saw the third row and the trunk of the Navigator. The SUV was a boat more than a car.

"How come you didn't get out the car?"

"I called shotgun and Dre been acting all funny style ever since, saying all sorts of dumb stuff like shotgun only works until Rome turns off the car."

"Lew, you know that-that-that's the rule," Dre growled.

I just smiled and could not stop shaking my head at the silliness of Dre and Lew. I think their silliness was what I enjoyed about them. They just didn't care what anyone thought.

"I've been dealing with this nonsense since I picked up Dre."

"This SUV is ridiculous," I said with a smile. I could not believe that Rome had a SUV, but not just a SUV a Lincoln Navigator.

"Yeah, my pops felt guilty about something and wanted to make me feel guilty too, I guess."

I laughed because I didn't pretend to understand the family drama that played out in any of my friends' homes. All I knew was Rome's dad worked a lot as a music producer. Rome had invited me over once and he showed me his dad's gold and platinum records and music studio in the basement of their house. His house was in the hills and overlooked the three bridges, the Bay Bridge, The Richmond Bridge and the Golden Gate Bridge, which connected the city with the Bay Area. The view was incredible.

"It's a million-dollar view," Rome said with a smile.

His mother, Missus Forrester, was this gorgeous woman who seemed so sweet. She looked like a model. It was hard to imagine her as a member of the Parent Teacher Association. She was always nice to me.

Lew lived with his mother near the island community of Alameda. His mother was a tech at one of the big internet companies. His dad was a doctor or physician. He did not talk too much about his family. They were always busy. I never had been to Lew's house. I only knew he lived near Alameda because he told me.

Dre had two older brothers, Larry and Eugene. Larry was in college. Eugene worked at Best Buy as a manager. He was a big schemer.

Dre had a love hate relation with his brothers. He loved Larry because he was at college. He hated Eugene because he still lived at home. Dre lived a few blocks from me, but he was closer to another school and preferred to hang in the neighborhood he grew up in. His dad had disappeared after Dre was born and left his mother to tend to three young boys. His mom worked for a non-profit and had a small business of her own.

Will and Dre were the only ones to ever come over to my house. Will was the only one to ever eat at my house. Our house was nice enough, but it wasn't a castle or McMansion. It suited us well. My mother worked at the Berkeley Farms Human Resources department and made sure to have food for us and that was enough for me. For an instant, I felt the pang of Will not being around.

I smiled. We were all friends. We were not perfect. There were times when we fought. There were times when we stopped talking with one another. It was a rollercoaster ride at times, but usually nothing threatened our friendship.

Rome drove and we talked as we drove and listened to music. Rome drove the SUV like an expert. The first stop was the hill above the zoo. The view was incredible because it looked east and west without restriction. To the east was the curve of trees which eventually led into the eastern valley Auggie rarely visited. To the west, from the hill, above the zoo, there was a view of, the Bay Bridge and the Richmond Bridge, two of the five bridges connecting the East Bay with the city by the bay.

Rome parked the Navigator and we all climbed out. Lew reluctantly climbed out of the SUV.

"Shotgun," Dre shouted as soon as Lew stood on the rail of the SUV.

"Man, you guys have to calm down. Everyone can sit shotgun. It's my Navi and I ain't about to have you fools rough housing in my ride. If you try that I'm going to pull over and leave you on the side of the road," Rome said. Dre and Lew stared at each other. "I mean it."

I smiled. I was not gunning for shotgun.

The two formed a truce and we sat on the Navi and admired the view. I smiled having been here before with BB.

"This must be a popular place to come," I said.

"Yeah," Rome said. "When my dad gave me the keys, he told me to go to three places. This was one of them."

"What were the other two," Lew asked.

"Jack London Square, by the Amtrak station," Rome said, thinking of what his father had suggested. "The other place is Lake Merritt. He says driving around the lake at night with the lights on the walkway is quite a sight."

I nodded. I looked at the sun still high in the blue sky overhead.

"So where do we go?"

"My dad has told me to only drive in the city limits until I get used to the Navi," Rome said. "He said after February I can drive on the freeways and whatnot."

"I think that's fair," I said with a smile. "I mean, we don't really go anywhere anyway."

"Yeah, you're right," Dre laughed.

Lew came in out of nowhere and bulled into the three of us. He was just a big kid. We wrestled a bit and then sat on the bumper of the Navigator and looked down onto the city below which seemed to outline the Bay in lights.

We drove around for an hour and drove to In 'N Out Burger and sat in line for burgers and fries. Rome told us we couldn't eat in the Navi for a week. He made us wait until he parked and made us eat outside of the Navi. He wanted to hold onto the new car smell for as long as possible. That seemed fair.

Things calmed down when Rome got the Navi. I stopped taking the bus. Rome picked me up on the way to school. It was like riding with BB all over, except it was Rome. Dre and I carpooled with Rome from January to the end of school, our sophomore year.

Lew was still getting a ride from his mother. His mother fought against Lew getting a ride from Rome for a full month. Then, unexpectedly, she gave in. During Black History month Lew was emancipated, sort of.

Lew as soon as he started riding with us could not stop telling us all he was going to get a car for his sixteenth birthday. Dre and I just shrugged off the comments. It didn't matter. Rome was sixteen and turning seventeen before all of us and had the Navi.

By February, the crew was liberated, thanks to Rome. Even though Rome had a Navigator the girls at Gee Dub kept their distance from us. It was sort of laughable. I decided to be magnanimous and sacrifice myself for the good of the team.

Black History month had begun, and the sophomore Valentine's Day Dance was just a week away. I had a conversation at the lunch table.

"I think there is the stench of rejection still on me," I told the three. "If you want to stand a chance of getting girls to pay attention, I suggest you cut me loose."

The three laughed at the idea.

"You know you might actually keep the crazy away," Lew said, with a chuckle spinning his empty milk carton on the table.

"Who's to say that we need these chicken heads?"

"Yeah, who's to say that-that-that we would do bet-bet-better without you," Dre smiled stabbing at his tater tots.

"You might be warding off all the psychos," Rome grinned with his food tray in front of him.

"Suit yourself," I said, with a shake of my head.

The Black History month committee were given the entire length of Gee Dub's main hall to display black achievements. There was an assembly scheduled at the end of the month. Speakers were going to be in the library once a week. Yet, it was the Cupid committee which was able to lobby for an annual Valentine's Day Dance in the gym. It was only one day, and no one objected.

Valentine's Day at Gee Dub was a big day in February. Well, the Valentine's Day Dance was the big event. During Black History month there was a night of dancing and public appearances of those smitten by others.

The week of Valentine's people received Valentine cards in each class. Some received candy. Some flowers. Faith gave each of us a Valentine's Day card. Every one of the crew gave Faith a Valentine's Day card. I think Rome gave her a box of chocolates. He was always doing too much.

In advisory Mister Pope decided to explain the significance of Valentine's Day with the story of wayward bird.

Rarely did Mister Pope spend any real amount of time in front of the advisory class, but that week, a few days before the Valentine's Day dance he told a slightly familiar Valentine's Day story.

"Okay, imagine you are a bird. You love being a bird. I mean, it's a pretty good life. You wake. You hunt for food. You sleep. You wake up. You eat some more. That's your life until you become old enough to start having urges." Pope paused. The boys elbowed each other. The girls shook their heads. "Hold on, here's my Valentine's Day problem. Imagine you are this bird, with urges, and you find yourself the only species of your kind suddenly somewhere else. Things are familiar because there are cliffs and fish and food and other birds, but no one that looks like you. You may have been thinking you were imagining things and then you realize something is wrong."

Mister Pope clicked a button and, on the screen, flashed a bird flying along the cliffside. It immediately looked like a seagull, but at the same time it didn't look like a seagull. The bird had a black tail and black tips on its wings. Its head was gray or black and had a long-blunted nose. The bird pinwheeled and flew back toward the camera. I swallowed.

Mister Pope was the teacher Mister Johnson talked about last year. All of a sudden, things seemed to snap into focus like never before. I looked at the video of the bird and recalled it was called gannet. I wanted to scream. I just wanted to scream realizing then and there my advisory teacher was Mister Pope, the very same teacher who had started my interest in a lost bird.

Mister Pope continued, "Now there are cliffs on both coasts. There's an ocean on either coast. I mean, you are a bird. You aren't the smartest creature on earth. Now, you, silly bird, find yourself the only bird like you on the west coast. No Valentine's Day for you."

Hands went up.

"How did it get here?" Sidney Tucker asked from behind her oversized glasses.

"No one knows," Mister Pope smiled.

"How come no one knows," Kevin Abbott asked.

"Well, there are a bunch of theories, but no one can be certain," Mister Pope said.

"So, there's only one of these birds on the west coast right now," Wendy Henderson asked.

"It's a gannet," Mister Pope said with a smile and nod.

"Why doesn't someone catch it and take it back," May Spooner asked in a tight sweater which showed off her curves.

"That's a good question, May," Mister Pope smiled.

"How come the bird people don't step in?" Hugh Drummer asked from his seat with a smirk.

"Wait, isn't there an organization in place that is supposed to protect animals?" May Spooner asked.

"This isn't a PETA problem," George Fellows sneered.

"There's this bird organization called Audubon," May pointed out looking at her cellphone. "How come they don't step in?"

"Well, it's just one bird," Mister Pope said.

"It doesn't seem fair," Edward Trumbull said.

"Welcome to Valentine's Day," Mister Pope smiled. "Not everyone gets all the chocolates, flowers and candy."

I was inspired after Mister Pope's anti-love speech cloaked in an anti-Valentine's Day lesson cloaked in Mo, the bird, who had somehow arrived on the west coast the only one of its kind.

In my History class I fished through my backpack and found a looseleaf notebook I had used only once. I looked through the first three pages and for the life of me had no idea what class I had scribbled the strange notes. I snatched out the three pages and had a new notebook for my newest project; saving Mo.

I rummaged in my backpack and found a Sharpie and drew a big M on the front of the notebook. I opened up the notebook and quickly wrote out the problem and the solution. Of course, the steps to get from the problem to the solution was the headache.

When class ended, I had a rough idea of the plan. It was filled with holes. I knew. I needed someone to look and bounce the ideas off and get some feedback.

"Faith, can I ask you a favor?"

"What?"

"Can you listen to this crazy idea and tell me what you think of it," I smiled.

Paris was eavesdropping and of course she was included in the conversation, though she had little to no input other than, "Really?" and "That's crazy."

My sophomore year I did not go to the Valentine's Day Dance. No one in the crew went to the Gee Dub social. Instead, Valentine's Day I called a meeting.

After school, we met. Dre looked exhausted. His last class of the day was PE with the football coach. The day before some boys got on the wrong side of the coach and as punishment the coach made everyone run for the whole period. Lew looked annoyed. His last class of the day was Science. Lew hated Science. "We are going to be tested on the Periodic Chart." Faith and Paris walked up wearing their gray windbreakers and sitting on the bleachers beside Dre. Faith's last class was History. Dre looked unusually uncomfortable. I couldn't help but smile. Rome was the last to arrive. He was all smiles. His last class of the day was Drama. He was preparing for the Black History month assembly. He was going to sing two songs. He was extremely excited.

"Sorry I am late," Rome smiled and seeing Faith, narrowed his dark eyes. "Auggie, who is this?"

"Everyone knows Faith. She went to Frederick Douglass with us."

"You know all these scrubs know us," Paris said with a lot of attitude.

Rome looked at Faith sitting on the bleachers with new eyes. He smiled.

"Oh, yeah, I remember you," Rome smirked.

"Yeah, I punched you once, so hard, you cried," Faith said with a slight smile.

I giggled and caught myself. Faith was no one to play with.

"You better recognize," said Paris, pouting.

I shook my head. Rome sat and Paris and he exchanged death stares.

"I think I have the community project to get behind," I said.

"Auggie, ain't nobody got time for this," Lew said. "I'm about to fail this Science test tomorrow."

"You ain't going to fail. We will help you," I said, meaning I would help Lew. "I'll call you tonight and give you some tips."

Lew took a deep breath.

"So, what are you thinking?"

"I'm thinking we are going to rescue that bird, You know the one we talked about last year," I said.

"What? I thought we thought it was too impossible."

"I've had a change of heart," I said. "I have been thinking and...and it seems doable."

"Auggie, don't take this the wrong way, but your idea of what is doable can be really dangerous," Rome smiled.

"The difference is that for this to work we will need to recruit a few people. We cannot do this alone. The best thing about letting the idea breath is that I have a better perspective now." I pulled out my M notebook. I showed them the mad scribbling in the pages.

"You losing your mind?"

"Not even," I said. "The way I see it we will need maybe about nine other people to make this happen."

"Nine other people?"

"Yeah, maybe twelve, but no more," Faith said.

Lew whistled. Dre rubbed his cheek, like he had been slapped. Rome sat on the bleachers with the number and mulled over the idea.

"Okay, give. What are you thinking?"

I detailed as much as I had planned. I told them straight out it was still a plan in planning. There were holes. My hope was for them to listen to the plan and to point out what I had missed.

We sat on the football bleachers for just under thirty minutes.

"Okay, the way I see this shaking out is that we start finding the most likely people to help us help them help that bird."

"Everyone that is in-in-interested in going to-to-to college will help," Dre said.

"This is a big ask," Lew said.

"Yeah, but the bigger the ask the bigger the reward," Paris smiled and stared at Rome like he stole something.

"So, we try and think of people that we can count on and bring them to the next meeting. We have to be sure that we can work with them. We can't have just anybody."

"Agreed."

"I think we need to go and see if we can find Mo," I said looking at Rome. Rome shook his head. He was the designated driver.

"Anything else?"

"Naw, that's it," I smiled. "Oh, wait, I think, well, Faith and I were talking about the project and I think we have a name for the group. The Rescuers."

Lew and Rome climbed off the bleachers. Dre and Paris smiled at each other. Lew and Rome seemed confused by Faith and Paris' presence. Faith waved and I waved. Faith and Paris walked back toward the main building.

The crew stopped me from leaving the football field.

"What gives, Auggie?"

I looked at the three looking at me. Dre was smiling like he had just learned he had a GameStop gift card. Lew was smirking, like he was about to lick his eyebrow. Rome, the most dramatic of us all crossed his arms in front of him and looked at me sideways, in a knowing way.

"She's got this supercomputer of a brain," I said. "I told her the idea and she just figured out things that I missed. She's the logistics person. She's also going to help us get people we can't get."

"Nothing else?"

"Nothing else," I said. "When I am interested, I will tell you. No sneak attacks."

"What about attitude Paris?"

"Nothing," I said. "You know they come as a pair."

With that everyone was onboard with Faith and Paris being a part of the Rescuers.

It's funny how things work out.

Faith and Paris became honorary members of the crew. Faith told me she might have a line on a financer and videographer but refused to give any details. Since her involvement the crew had been focused and trying to figure out ways to take the plan from paper to reality.

On the first Saturday in March, the crew called and told me to be ready to go by noon. I was the last person picked up and climbed in the rear of the SUV and smiled seeing Lew sitting, sulking, in the second row with me.

"What happened?"

"I asked Rome to-to-to pick me up first," Dre in a dressed in a Gee Dub windbreaker smiled from the passenger seat. Rome just shook his head as he pulled the Navigator into traffic.

I laughed. Lew sulked dressed in a hooded sweatshirt and jeans until we climbed on the freeway. Before we got to the freeway, I explained that if we were going to have any chance of seeing Mo it would be at Half Moon Bay or Devil's Slide.

"Why you saying that?"

"Well, I did some research. The Farrallon Islands are only accessible by the ferry once we get there. I don't think that I accounted for the ferry in the plan. We have to have some freedom to get in and get out. The ferry means a schedule." I paused. "So, we should head to Half Moon Bay first."

Dre punched in the directions on the dashboard and the SUV gave us turn-by-turn directions to Half Moon Bay. The trip was under forty miles and just about an hour from Oakland.

"When we get there, we have to stop and eat," Lew said as we hurtled down the freeway toward the south Bay.

"Food sounds good," I admitted.

We crossed the Dumbarton bridge and zipped past Facebook Headquarters on the way to Half Moon Bay. The trip was pretty smooth. Rome was a great driver. He loved his new toy.

"So, how do you think we find out where Mo hangs out?"

"I'm sure some locals there will know," I said. "I mean, it might be a tourist attraction."

We exited the freeway and instantly felt the lack of diversity in the beach town. As we made our slow climb over a winding two lane road most of the passengers coming down looked nothing like us. I noted the beachfront at the top of the hill with a number of hidden driveways which led to private homes hidden on the hill. We followed the traffic down the other side of the hill to a four-lane highway which brought us to what was Half Moon Bay.

"Where do we go?"

"Follow the signs to the cliffs," I said, looking out the window. "Hopefully, we can eat along the way."

Lew and Dre were looking out the window, just like Rome and me. We drove the posted speed limit as we slid down the hill into the quiet of Half Moon Bay.

"Remember, stop at the first place you see to get something to eat," Lew said and as the words issued out of his mouth Rome signaled and turned left and cut across the two lanes of oncoming traffic. He pulled the Navigator into the parking lot of the burger stand which looked like it would be something found in the fifties. Rome parked in the parking lot and we climbed out of the SUV and I immediately stretched my legs and arms. Lew climbed out and pushed past Rome to the window to order.

Dre and Rome followed behind Lew. I looked around and noted the lack of sidewalks on the main street. That seemed odd to me. I mean, didn't every town have sidewalks?

As I closed the Lincoln's door, I noticed the stares of some in the cars as they passed. Most of the drivers did not look like us. I smiled at the looks and slowly turned to my friends who were ordering their food.

"What you getting, Auggie?"

"I suppose a cheeseburger, fries and a fruit punch," I said looking at the short menu above the window.

Dre and Rome laughed. Lew was standing to the side filming the quiet main street of Half Moon Bay.

"What's so funny?"

"I bet Dre that you would order a cheeseburger, fries and a drink," Rome chuckled.

"I said a ham-ham-hamburger, fries and a drink," Dre smiled.

"I'm that predictable?"

"Yeah," Dre grinned.

"Did you ask about Mo?"

Rome and Dre looked at each other silently.

I spun around and walked to the window. The counter worker was a dark-haired white girl wearing a hairnet and a gray T-shirt with a nametag that read: Sabrina. Behind her I watched two other women, in their forties, at the small grill. They had on hairnets as well and gray T-shirts. They also wore white aprons. A short, potbellied man who looked like he might be part bulldog was stacking boxes of vegetables in a corner of the burger stand.

"Can I help you?"

"Yes, hi," I said. "I already ordered. I was wondering if you know anything about the bird that got lost here?"

Sabrina's thin dark eyebrows dived in as she looked at me like I had spoken a language she had never heard before. She leaned back and smiled, parting her thin lips and showing her crooked teeth. Sabrina placed her elbow on the counter and tilted her head as if doing so might make her understand what I had said better. The counter worker rested her head on her fist.

"You know, the bird that is not supposed to be here?"

"You mean Morris?"

I smiled. I nodded. I felt instantly stupid. I should have led with that.

"Well, I think there's a tour down by the cliff. You just have to go up one of the hills and you will see the signs," Sabrina said. She added, "I have never seen him, but not everyone does, I suppose."

"Thanks," I said and walked to the three, who were waiting for their food.

"Well, what did you find out Sherlock?"

I shook my head. "There's a tour. We just have to go up the hill and we'll see it," I said.

Our food arrived and Rome insisted on sitting at the table and eating. He didn't care if people stared. He ate. Lew and Dre ate. I ate but watched the streets for more of us in Half Moon Bay. In the ten or fifteen minutes it took for us to eat our food and drink our drinks I saw maybe five people who looked remotely like us. They weren't white, but they weren't black either. It was a weird feeling.

Half Moon Bay should have been called the Other Side of the Moon for me.

After we finished eating, we climbed back in the Navigator and headed for the hills and the cliffside. We didn't have too far to drive. After about ten minutes we found ourselves in a parking lot. Rome parked and paid the maximum amount of time, two hours.

"Okay, let's find this tour," Rome said.

Lew led the way. Dre, Rome and I followed. I found myself noticing people looking at us as we walked toward the cliffside. We followed the signs. There was a professional looking sign that read: Morris Tours Daily.

We followed the string of signs to a leathery man wearing sandals and board shorts. The man's skin looked like a saddlebag more than like skin. He was sitting in one of those cheaply made chaise lounges.

"Excuse me," Lew said as we stopped behind him. "Is the tour happening today?"

The man, behind a pair of dark sunglasses jerked awake at Lew's words. He had blonde hair that was shaved on the sides. Around his neck was a shark tooth necklace. The leathery man climbed to his sandaled feet and stuck his index fingers under his shades and rubbed at his eyes. He had thin leathery lips and a nearly invisible chin.

"Hey, what's up, gentlemen," the leathery stranger smiled, showing his white teeth. "Sorry, was catching a few zees. Been walking up and down the cliffs today. Been a long day."

I checked my phone and noted it was only two o'clock.

"So, can we see the bird?"

"Can you take us to see Morris," Rome asked.

"Yeah," said Dre.

"Sure, gentlemen," the tall and bony leathery stranger smiled. "I want to point out that I cannot control Morris. He is a free spirit. He likes to fly around here in the afternoons. He goes north a lot. But that is usually during the later hours. We still have some daylight. So, we should catch sight of him today, but I cannot guarantee he will be flying. I can just find him." The leathery tour guide pointed to the sign. The tour was twenty dollars a person. The guide smiled, "If you don't see anything, I'll give you half your money back," the guide smiled.

Rome paid for the tour.

We walked to the cliffside. We all had our phones out and recording. I was looking for things to add to the plan.

The trek up the hill from the parking lot was only about three minutes.

"Hey, what's your name?"

"I'm Jay," the stranger said from behind his sunglasses. He was moving at a leisurely pace but the trail he had us on was not easy or simple. It, the trail, seemed more suited to goats than people. We twisted and out of the blue were near the cliff edge.

Now, the idea of a cliffside in theory is the edge of the land which gives way to the sea. I thought that as I followed the bony leathery stranger.

"Damn," Lew said, daring to look over the edge. He immediately took two steps to the left to insure his safety.

"Be careful," Jay said. "We are going to head to the Vista Point first and then to The Hook. Morris likes flying around there."

I looked to the sea and saw the vastness of the ocean which seemed to go on forever. The only thing to stop it was the horizon itself. I had lived in the Bay Area all my life and never been to the ocean.

The Pacific Ocean was this incredible force of nature. I looked at it to the right of us and tried to imagine how high we were. I looked back and noticed the parking lot was a distant memory. On the top of the rise, I could see why people drove to the beach. It was beautiful. It had to be incredibly peaceful at sunrise or sunset.

"Come on, guys, we are not that far from Vista Point," Jay smiled and gestured us to follow the goat trail along the edge of the cliff.

"Hey, shouldn't there be a fence or something along the edge of this trail," Rome said as he walked behind Lew and in front of Dre.

"I was thinking the same thing," Lew said. "This place has to be super dangerous at night."

"Naw," Jay grunted. "Most people that come up here know what they are facing. They ain't too many tourists that walk around here at night."

Jay walked us another five minutes to a stretch of land that reminded me of a tabletop. It was the most level bit of land we had traversed up until that point. There was a railing around the bit of lip that jutted from the cliff. The Vista Point was maybe twenty-five feet wide and as long.

Jay waved us onto the tabletop and walked to the railing and shielded his eyes to the sun and looked out toward the ocean. We all followed Jay to the rail and looked at the sea below. I looked down and felt my stomach tighten just a bit. I reached out and grabbed the handrail. I closed my eyes for a moment and tried to breathe.

"Look north and south, Morris is usually sitting in the rocks in the cliffside. If he ain't in the rocks he's flying around looking for food."

"You okay," Dre asked, placing a hand on my shoulder.

I nodded. I opened my eyes. I did not look down. I looked out at the waves and the sea foam which broke up the dark water and waves.

"Is that it," Lew asked, pointing toward me. "Is that Mo?"

I followed his index finger and looked at a cliff wall where there were easily a dozen birds. I looked at the white birds on the cliffside and there to the side of the seagulls was a gray headed bird which seemed a little bigger than the others.

"Damn," Rome breathed. "There it is."

"See," said Jay. "You get your money's worth on this tour."

We all took pictures and video of Mo. Lew took pictures of us at Vista Point. We asked Jay to take a picture of us on the railing of Vista Point with the ocean in the background. All in all, it had taken two hours to accomplish everything on our trip to Half Moon Bay.

Jay walked us back to the top of the parking lot where we had found him.

"How come you know so much about this bird," Lew asked.

"I got time on my hands," Jay said as he walked us down the goat trail. "The bird ain't that smart, you know? They got these small bird brains. So, they just do the things they know. So, Morris, he is happy to come here in the middle of the day. I guess he must be at the Farrallons earlier. I know that I've seen him head north before sunset. So, I suppose he rests there during the night." Jay smiled. "It ain't rocket science."

"Yeah," Dre agreed. Lew and Rome agreed.

I was not so certain.

Rome unlocked the Navigator and we piled back in. Rome started the SUV and reversed out of the parking lot. In a few minutes we were back on the main strip of Half Moon Bay.

"Hey, before we hit the road, I'm getting some gas. If you got to use it, then use it while I get some gas," Rome said.

The Lincoln rolled easily down the main street and Rome turned into the first gas station. It was one of those gas stations that pretends to be a shopping mall as well. Rome pulled up in front of a gas pump and we offered to chip in for gas. Rome wouldn't hear of it.

"It gives my dad something to talk about with me," Rome laughed.

Lew and Dre headed into the gas station. I lingered by the Navigator.

"Rome, thanks for doing all this," I said.

"Sure, man, we all trying to go to college," Rome smiled.

"Yeah, but you ain't got to worry about the money like the rest of us," I said.

"Don't know about all that," Rome admitted. "My pops got money, but he can be funny style about it. Everything has a cost connected to it." He said pumping the gas in the SUV. "Like this gift is not a no strings attached gift. It's a write off." Rome smiled. "Nothing is free in this world," he said with a shake of the head.

"How do you mean?"

"He holds this over me. He writes it off, no biggie, but it's a way to constantly prove he cares," Rome said, holding the gas pump nozzle. "It's a bit twisted."

I nodded. I didn't pretend to understand. Families were complicated, even the best of them.

"Hey, I'm going to pay a water bill," Rome said as Lew and Dre came walking out of the gas station. "If you got to go you should go now."

I nodded. Rome headed for the gas station. I watched the gas pump numbers ticking up to fill up the Navigator. If it was under sixty dollars I would be surprised.

"We got some snacks," Lew barked as Rome passed. I smiled as Lew lifted his bag of goodies.

I thought about Rome's suggestion. I figured it was only an hour until we returned home. I could hold it if I needed.

I was weighing the whole wait or go when a Half Moon Bay police car pulled into the gas station. Lew and Dre were horsing around near the SUV when the two policemen climbed out of the patrol car and one walked into the store and the other looked in our direction.

I watched the policeman watching us. Instantly, I regretted not going to the bathroom. I took a deep breath and turned to Lew and Dre who were busy bothering each other.

"Hey, look up, we are being watched," I said.

Lew and Dre went from carefree to concerned, instantly. Lew, dressed in a hooded sweatshirt and baggy jeans and Kobe basketball sneakers peeked around the SUV in the direction of the gas station. Dre, dressed in a long-sleeved Oaklandish T-shirt, Gee Dub windbreaker and blue jeans poked his head in the direction Lew was looking.

"What they want with us?"

"No telling," I said, not taking my eyes off the crew cut white policeman standing beside his cruiser, dressed in the dark blue long-sleeved uniform with a bulletproof vest underneath, making his chest thicker than usual. Over his heart was a shiny badge. The man was one of those square-faced, thin lipped, mustached, police guys who dressed for all-out war on the streets of Half Moon Bay. On his waist was a gun and a taser. He was wearing tactical gloves and his thumbs were hooked beneath the bulletproof vest. His eyes were hidden behind reflective sunglasses.

"Should we be-be-be worried," asked Dre.

"I don't think so," I said. "They probably trying to intimidate us," I said, looking around the gas station and noting there were a dozen gas pumps but only about half being used.

"So, what do we do?"

"Well, I want to go to the bathroom all of a sudden, but--"

"You should go," Lew said.

"Yeah," said Dre.

"If they are going to bother us or whatever you might as well not have that messing with you at the same time."

"Yeah, we-we-we got enough to-to-to deal with, let alone you pee-pee-peeing on yourself," Dre said with a slight smirk.

"Well, the pump should shut off in a minute, I was sort of waiting for Rome or someone else to watch the gas," I explained and shook my head. I looked back at Lew and Dre and then back to the store where Rome was just leaving. I pushed away from the Navigator and headed to the main building.

Behind Rome stepped the other police officer. He was watching Rome as he walked from the storefront and I approached. I watched the policeman watching Rome and out of the corner of my eye watched the other Half Moon Bay officer who remained by the patrol car.

"Everything okay?" I asked.

"Yeah," Rome said, and I knew he saw the police activity at the gas station.

"I decided to go to the bathroom before we head out," I said as I passed Rome and nearly ran into the tall white policeman standing in front of the double doors of the gas station.

"Watch yourself there, son," the thin-lipped policeman said, a tall man dressed in the same dark blue uniform, with a shiny badge over his heart. I stopped long enough to register the gun, the taser, the three blue stripes on his shirt's long-sleeve cuff and the nameplate which read: Roberts. Roberts was clean shaven, older, with hints of gray in his blonde crew cut. His eyes were hidden behind mirror framed sunglasses which sat on his thin and pointed nose.

I didn't respond. I thought to respond but I immediately had more important things to deal with. Once in the store, I looked to the cashier, a fat faced man wearing a collared shirt behind a counter, and then scanned the interior of the store for the bathroom. There were maybe three or four people in the store. Seeing the sign, I was looking for, I headed toward the bathroom. The sooner I relieved myself, the sooner we could leave Half Moon Bay.

Finding the bathroom, I stepped in and did all I needed. I washed my hands and stepped back into the store proper. The cashier, helping a customer, watched me as I left the store heading for the SUV at the pump.

When I stepped out of the store Lew and Dre were standing on the side of the Navigator with the mustached policeman standing beside them and Rome talking to the taller policeman. Instantly, I took out my phone and pressed the camera app and flipped to video and began recording.

"What is going on?" I asked.

"This your friend," the mustached cop asked Lew and Dre. Lew was looking at the tops of his shoes. Dre was doing the same.

"Why you bothering my friends?" I asked the officer.

The policeman closest to Lew and Dre turned his dark sunglasses in my direction and I paused, preparing for whatever was to come.

"Young man, can you turn off that camera?"

"Why?" I asked.

"Because I asked you," the policeman talking to Rome said. "Stay right there," the policeman said to Rome and he stepped toward me. Seeing the policeman move toward me I stopped.

"No," I said loudly. "Can you tell me what is the problem, officer?"

I was not within arm's reach of either officer. I quickly scanned the gas station for help. A few people seemed curious what was happening. A couple of people stood beside their cars and pulled out their cell phones and looked at the activity at the gas pump. I smiled.

"I want to point out that you saw me earlier go into the store. You did not need to talk to me then. So, there shouldn't be a real need to talk to me now."

The taller policeman smiled one of those smiles which look friendly but is anything but.

"Just curious what brought you to our fair city, today," the taller officer said, handing Rome back his papers.

"Do you ask everyone that comes to your fair city why they are visiting," I asked, feeling anger rising in me. "Or did you decide that we didn't seem to fit in your fair city?"

"What's your name, young man?"

"Why?" I asked.

"Again, because I asked."

"I am a minor. I was taught by my mother not to give my name to people I don't know," I said. I added, "If you want to know my name you can call my mother and talk to her. I am sure she would want to know why you, officer Roberts, decided to harass me and my friends on a Saturday afternoon in Half Moon Bay."

Roberts smiled. He looked like he was weighing out his options. The mirror glasses held my gaze but then I saw the glasses move a little to the left and right. Lew and Dre kept their heads down. Rome was still in front of the Navigator.

I continued to record.

"Can you tell me why you were harassing my friends, officer? It seems that of all the people in this gas station you focused on, why did you just decide to harass us. Why did you feel you had to know all our information?"

"You have a nice day," Roberts said finally. He and his partner walked from the Navigator and I gave them a lot of space. I did not stop recording until the two policemen had reached their patrol car.

I looked and saw my voice had drawn the attention of about three or four others. They had their phones out too. They were talking amongst themselves.

I turned back to the crew and the Navigator.

"What the hell just happened?" Rome said and gave me a hug.

Lew and Dre looked at each other and then hugged me too. Rome walked around the front of the SUV and climbed in. We all climbed into the SUV and Rome started the Navigator and shook his head. I kept looking back at the police. Lew and Dre shook their heads. Dre looked back with me to watch the police sitting in their car.

"What do we do?"

"What do you mean," I said. "We get up out of Half Moon Bay." I paused. "Don't do anything to get a ticket. Keep the Navi under the speed limit."

Rome nodded. He put the Lincoln in gear and pulled out of the gas station.

"Everyone phones out, just in case."

We rode out of Half Moon Bay with a police car following us up the hill and down the hill and to the freeway exit. I recorded it all.

When we found the freeway, I was already thinking what to do next. The SUV was quiet. As we looked around and saw people driving cars who looked like us everyone in the Navigator seemed to relax.

"Where did that come from, Auggie," Lew asked, sitting on the second row of the Lincoln.

I shrugged.

Dre leaned forward and pulled me by my shoulders.

"I'm glad you were there-there-there," Dre managed.

I shrugged out of Dre's grip.

"That was some other level stuff."

"Not really," I said. "My mom always tells me how to deal with oppressors. We have to continue watching them. They do evil things when they think they are not being watched or held accountable."

The SUV slid down the freeway and everyone just relived the whole situation all over again. The policeman who had followed Rome out of the store kept following him when I went into the store. He asked Rome if the Navigator was his car. He asked to see Rome's license and registration. While the other cop walked up, with his hand on his gun grip, and asked Lew and Dre what they were doing in Half Moon Bay. To their credit, Lew and Dre did not say anything.

"Have to admit I wanted to say something," Lew began.

"You? Me too, but Aug-Aug-Augie's mom told me the same-same-same thing."

"So, we just waited him out."

"He asked us our names and I told him Smith and Jones," Lew smiled.

"He asked for ID," Dre said.

"I told them we were minors and didn't have ID. We didn't have to have ID. That's the law," Lew said, trying to sound like he gave the cop as good as the cop gave them.

I shook my head. All I recalled of the situation was the sight of Lew and Dre sitting on the railing of the Navi and Rome at the front grill. I closed my eyes to the memory.

"So, are we going to drive by Devil's Slide?"

"What? No," Rome said, dejected.

"I thought the plan was to go to Half Moon Bay and then to swing by Devil's Slide?"

"Yeah, I don't know about this whole rescue thing, Auggie," Rome said, his confidence shaken.

"Yeah, Auggie, they don't want-want-want us in their ci-ci-cities," Dre stammered.

I looked in the rear of the Navi and looked at Lew. He was the Tree-Hugger.

"I don't know, man, if they don't want us around it is going to be almost impossible to save that bird."

"What? You guys forgot how we get treated in Oakland?" I looked at Dre and Lew and then Rome. "They can't win. They can't dictate to us." I sat there and tried not to get angry. I closed my eyes. "There's nowhere they want us. We are uninvited guests to them that have overstayed our welcome. But that ain't on us. We're here now. They have to deal with it. They have to accept it."

"What if they don't?"

I didn't answer.

"So, can we swing by Devil's Slide?"

"No, I'm not feeling it. I'm heading back to..."

"Places you feel comfortable?"

"Yeah, there's nothing wrong with that," Rome said.

The ride back to the Oakland was quieter than the ride out to Half Moon Bay. There was a heaviness hanging over the SUV. I wanted to shake them and make them understand my point of view, but it seemed pointless.

I sat in the passenger seat of the Navigator and watched as the cities on the freeway signs fell away and eventually became those announcing the airport, downtown and the familiar exit which led to my home.

"Thanks," I said as I climbed out of the Navigator.

I stood on the sidewalk and tried to think of my next step.

Chapter 14.

March- April

The Tuesday after our trip to Half Moon Bay, Rome picked me up and the Navi was real quiet. I said, "Hey," and everyone nodded or grunted but did not really engage. I didn't care or see it as a big deal for the Navi to be quiet. Rome was playing "Rockstar" as we pulled away from the curb. I just listened to the music. It was early and I didn't have too much to say that morning. I just rode to school trying to figure out the master plan and all the school daily workload.

We arrived at school and it seemed as if the trio were a little tender for some reason beyond me. I gave Rome, Lew and Dre a little space. There were always times when one of the group wasn't interested in talking. I supposed there had to be times when we all just didn't have anything to talk about. It was not something I imagined happened often, but I chalked the weird morning up to the weird Tuesday morning.

"See you at lunch," I said and headed to my Advisory class.

They tiptoed around me as if I was made of glass for some reason. Well, they seemed to be made of glass and they were afraid of me breaking them. They shot me side glances and at lunch, but they did not want to talk much.

"How are the applications going," I asked Dre, curious. It was a softball question.

He smiled and nodded, but that was about all.

When I asked Rome and Lew about their classes, they didn't have much to say.

"Everything's good, Auggie," Lew said, reluctantly.

I was suddenly angry at all of them for making me feel like I had done something wrong. I wanted to flip over the table or swipe all the trays and food off the table, like I had seen in movies and TV shows. I looked down and saw some milk cartons and a tray with a partial eaten pear and salad on the table. It wasn't enough.

"Well, I know it's not, and y'all are acting like I did something, and I know I didn't," I said at the lunch table.

Rome looked away. Dre did too.

"What gives?"

"We were talking about what happened at Half Moon Bay," Lew said.

I listened. I wanted to know what they had talked about.

"I guess, we knew it happened, but we just didn't expect it to happen at Half Moon Bay."

"Hell, man, that stuff happens everywhere not just at Half Moon Bay," I said with a smile. "It happens every day with a y in it, my mom told me." I paused. "Welcome to America with the triple K."

Rome and Dre looked down at the table.

"What's wrong with y'all?"

"I had some time to think about it," Rome began. "I just didn't believe that it was that bad."

Dre just shook his head.

"Look Auggie, you are the brains of the group," Lew said. "Everyone's got a role. Me, I am the conscious of the group. You get it?"

"I get it, Lew," I said. "But I think y'all are overthinking the situation. It happened. We lived through it. We move on."

"But, I don't know if we want to move on," Rome said.

"You sort of flipped things upside down when we went to Half Moon Bay," Lew said. "Things are all, I don't know, unsettled."

"How," I asked. "I mean, you are the only ones that care about roles. I just was trying to protect my friends. Nothing else."

Dre and Rome were pretending to eat but paying attention. Lew twisted his lips before he continued.

"We are all trying to figure things out, Auggie," Lew said.

"I mean, what-what-what are we doing trying to-to-to rescue a bird when things are so messed up in our own back-back-backyard?"

Rome and Lew nodded in agreement. I had an inkling of the problem instantly. I nodded. I took a moment to gather my thoughts before I spoke.

"What we talking about is making a difference. The problem is that we get this crazy idea that what we see in Oakland is everywhere, but it ain't," I said. "Life ain't Gee Dub. Life is what is going on at all those white private schools with the three black teachers and six black custodians and security guards." I felt my anger growing. "But the only way to change things is to prove their ignorance and racism is wrong."

"How?"

I didn't answer for a long moment.

"We cannot let them scare us into just being athletes, entertainers and drug dealers," I said. "We can be so much more." I tried to think of the right words. "Remember when we talked about the Bill Gates Millenium Award and y'all said you were going to apply. You should. We should. They have limited our dreams. They have lowered our expectations. One of you could be the first, but that ain't gonna happen if we don't try. We can't knock down the doors that are locked and barred for us without one of us having the key to those locks."

"Auggie, you are--," Rome started.

"Militant," Lew said.

"No, I think that I am just starting to wake up." I looked around the cafeteria.

"What are you talking about?"

I didn't answer Rome. I looked at my friends and thought before I spoke. "What we do could inspire someone else with rescuing their own Mo."

"Just one Mo," said Lew.

I shook my head.

"Naw, man, just one Morus Bassanus. There are so many Mos to be discovered and rescued."

Dre smiled.

"Things are still...," Rome trailed off.

I nodded.

"Things don't change because of happy thoughts," I said. "Things change because people see the problem and want to change it. We can't let someone who doesn't know us limit our dreams. If we do that then they win. We aren't saving Mo for them. We are saving Mo for us. We are saving Mo because they can't and we can." I paused. "We are saving this bird to show what we are capable of despite the box they want to put us in."

Lew, Dre and Rome looked at me blankly.

At the bell I climbed to my feet and left the three. Lunch ended and I headed to Math class.

After Math, I ran into Faith and Paris in the hallway on my way to Science. They did not look happy to see me. I waved and thought the two staring daggers at me was over. It wasn't.

Paris stepped into my way and threw out her hip and pressed her fingers together like she was about to snap. I stopped in the hallway. Paris pointed toward Faith who looked mad against the lockers. I looked down the hall to where my Science class was and back at Paris.

"Don't do that," Paris said, stepping back and against the lockers where Faith was staring at me like her eyes could cut me to mincemeat.

"So, I heard you decided to take on the Half Moon Bay police force?"

"What," I said to Faith and Paris. Paris stood behind me, making sure I could not continue to my class. I had no idea Faith or Paris cared about what happened at Half Moon Bay.

"How I'm going to find out from Dre's 'gram?"

"Yeah, I thought you guys were talking on the regular," Paris smirked.

"That all happened on Saturday and I got mad at them because they refused to go to Devil's Slide afterward. So, I just went home, turned off my phone and ate and watched Netflix. The next day I didn't wake up until late. Then it was Monday."

Paris pushed the back of my head. I spun around immediately angry. The girl with the long straight black hair pouted and dared me to do something. I looked at her light brown eyes.

"Now, you know how we felt when we learned that you nearly got Ahmaud Arbery'd." Faith said.

"Or George Floyd or Breonna Taylor'd," Paris said.

"It wasn't like that," I tried.

"Auggie, that was bad form," Paris smirked. "That's all I'm saying. If you get involved with the po-po you need to tell everyone. It's the only way to be protected nowadays."

"It wasn't like that," I said, knowing Paris wasn't listening.

Faith crossed her arms in front of her and poked out her lower lip. She didn't say much. I didn't know what I was supposed to say after Paris's comments.

"Well, we still meeting today, after school?"

"Yeah," I said. "On the bleachers, after school."

Faith and Paris hearing that spun on their heels and walked toward their classes. I walked away and tried to get to class before the tardy bell.

After Art I headed to the football field. There were a knot of people near the gym and I pushed through and toward the front of the school. The Gee Dub security officers were walking toward me as I headed up the hall.

One of the Gee Dub security officers was officer Darryl, a friendly giant, with Mohawk and beard, who usually patrolled the lunchroom or the parking lot during school hours. He was also an assistant coach on the track team.

"What's going on," I asked as Darryl and Miss Rita, the other security officer seemed laser focused. Not really concerned I passed the security officers and reached the front of the school. I did not stop at the office or wave to anyone. I just walked out the front door and down the stairs to the football field.

On the football bleachers, the Rescuers assembled. As I walked the few remaining feet to the bleachers, I was not surprised to find a few new faces. Sitting and talking on the bleachers were Faith and Paris. Next to them was Tanza Smith, one of the social elites of Gee Dub. I had said maybe a dozen words to the Gee Dub celebrity in the two years I had been at the high school. She was on another level. If the rumors were to be believed her dad was one of the Bay Area's rap legends. Next to Tanza Smith was this round-faced girl I had seen but never talked to before. On the other side of Tanza Smith was a long-limbed boy dressed in a monogrammed long-sleeve collared shirt and tailored khaki pants. I had seen monogrammed clothes before but the thing which caught my eye was his monogrammed custom-made Nikes.

In front of the bleachers was this spidery kid wearing a backpack and carrying a pretty professional camera and filming.

As I reached the bleachers Faith snapped to attention. Paris turned toward me. Faith cleared her throat and Tanza Smith cut her eyes toward me. With Tanza's action and semi-attention all the others, including the oval-faced girl, the monogram boy and the amateur videographer sat and looked at me.

"Hey, everyone," I began a little unsure. I wondered where the crew were. I began the second Rescuers meeting.

I ripped through the idea of getting everyone into college and explained the plan, again in broad strokes. Faith smiled and nodded and continued to encourage. I learned everyone's name who was sitting on the bleachers that afternoon.

I met Tanza Smith, Cash Money Graham, Quincy "Cue" Pierce and Derricka Monroe. Faith had talked to them all and invited them to the Rescuers. I was surprised to see Tanza and Cash in the crew. They had to have enough money to go to any college they wanted.

Tanza Smith was the Gee Dub celebrity who arrived in a chauffeur driven car and was picked up in the same. Tanza was very attractive for a sixteen-year-old. She had shoulder length curly black hair, a big forehead, broad nose and uneasy smile. Dressed like the other girls Tanza's clothes looked a little newer and gave the impression of being the highest quality. On her ears sat four diamond studs which easily weighed two carats. On her wrist she wore a watch I swore I had seen in a rap video. On her feet were limited-edition basketball sneakers. Her backpack was Burberry. Everything about Tanza suggested excess.

The round-face girl was Derricka Monroe. She was an aspiring social media content manager. In other words, she was always on social media trying to be an influencer. Derricka was somehow connected to Tanza. Either she was her blood cousin or a close friend. I never really knew which.

The long-limbed boy with the bored bad boy feeling about him was Cash Money Graham. He was the son of the one-time street hustler turned rapper Rock-A-Fella. His father had become famous for his raps but become extremely wealthy suing and successfully winning a dozen lawsuits against rappers who dared tried to use his signature beats on their records without his permission. Cash was a slacker but driven to do better than his father.

He wore monogrammed everything the first time I met him. He seemed a little like Rome, seeking attention. Cash Money Graham was a schemer, plotter and corner cutter. He was incredibly smart and only used just enough of his brain to keep his grades high. As he sat in the bleachers, I figured he might be the biggest problem or the easiest to deal with because he was either on or off when doing something.

The videographer was Cue. He wanted to be a documentary filmmaker. His mother was a documentarian. She had done a number of documentaries and was working on editing a Black Lives Matter documentary she had finished in 2021. Cue's hope was to go to USC Film School. He was going to use the footage of the rescue of Mo as an entry into USC. Based on the plan Cue was one hundred percent in. He only asked to be at every meeting.

About ten minutes after the meeting started Lew and Dre showed up. A few minutes later Rome appeared. Rome, Lew and Dre were unexpectedly hesitant. The idea of rescuing a bird seemed such a small and meaningless thing in the face of what had happened in Half Moon Bay.

At the end of the second Rescuers meeting the three friends who had been so supportive of the project pulled me aside. Faith and Paris watched, discreetly near enough to hear the conversation.

"Auggie, I don't know," Lew said.

Rome started to speak and went silent, thinking.

"I mean," Dre started.

Cash and Tanza stepped forward, looking at the trio.

"Listen, you don't have to do nothing you ain't comfortable with," Tanza smiled, showing off her perfectly straight teeth.

"We are here to stay, Auggie," Cash said, cutting his eyes toward the crew. "We are going to see this through to the end. If there's money involved, that's icing on the cake."

I tried to quiet everyone down.

"I think you don't get it," I said. "We don't have any control of how those people see us or treat us. They have so much anger and hate inside," I tried. "They just hate to hate." I shook my head. "I don't understand them. If I had a choice, I wouldn't try to understand them. I don't have that choice. None of us do. So, we have to get along with them." I took a breath. "We all have failed. We have all stumbled. But, to me, rescuing that bird, who has no one to help it back to its kind, is a way to show them all they have misjudged us. They underestimate us. We are smart. We are ingenious. We are more than what they think or know of us." Cue was filming. I shook my head and finished by saying, "Before we are done, we are going to prove to everyone we can do more."

"I'm sold," said Rome, with a shake of his head.

Lew and Dre were not convinced.

"We're in, Auggie," Faith said, putting an arm around Tanza's shoulder. Tanza and Paris nodded.

Lew and Dre seemed to be weighing out the new development.

Involving others seemed to take the pressure off my shoulders. It was a good and bad thing. It was good because I didn't have to carry all the weight and responsibility. It was a bad thing, in my mind, because I couldn't control every aspect of the plan. I just had to figure out the details. Lew and Dre's hesitation didn't matter. The new edition of the Rescuers pushed on.

Four weeks after the first new edition of the Rescuers meeting, I was pulled out of the hall by Paris and Tanza and rushed to the front office where Faith and Cash were waiting. Cue was hot on our heels.

"Auggie, just been working out the details of the plan," Faith said as we sat on the chairs just outside of the office, like we were waiting to go in. Students who walked by assumed we were in trouble.

"Listen, I'm all in but there seems to be too many unknowns for me and Cash to be in this amateur hour."

"What we need is a real solid plan."

"Maybe, you can tighten this up."

"If you can't tighten things up then we may have to cut our losses," Cash finally said, bored.

I listened. I nodded. I understood.

"Give me until the end of the month," I said. I had an option I had been holding out on for just such a situation.

"End of the month," Tanza said.

Paris and Faith remained as the others walked away after the ambush.

"Together we can figure this whole thing out. We just have to work together," Faith said.

Faith sat next to me. Paris pouted.

"I suppose this is on me," I said.

All that information was swimming in my head when I decided to walk in on Mister Pope and sit with him for lunch and pick his brain. I figured of everyone on campus Mister Pope was the most knowledgeable and passionate about Mo, the gannet.

"Mister Pope, can I ask you a question," I said walking into the quiet classroom of my Advisory teacher. Pope was on the far side of the classroom and straightening up some books. He was methodically placing books under some desks. I quickly looked around and noted the dozen books sitting on the desks. I immediately started putting the books under the desks, so Mister Pope didn't have as much work to do.

Mister Pope seeing me putting the books under the desk stopped and smiled. He walked to his desk and grabbed his lunch from his mini fridge. He sat at his desk as I finished putting the books under the desk.

"What brings you here, during lunch, August?"

"I just was curious how come no one has tried to save the bird and return it back to its kind?"

I sat down in front of my Advisory teacher and secretly tapped my phone's voice recorder.

Chapter 15.

April-May

After Spring break, we had our most important Rescuers meeting ever. Everyone was there. There were eight of us sitting in the conference room of the office Tanza had arranged for our meeting. It was raining outside like Noah had built an ark somewhere.

"Okay, as promised, I went and talked to Mister Pope before we went to Spring break and he had some important information. Of course, he didn't know that he was helping us with the rescue. I think that he just thought he was teaching me something I didn't know."

"Okay, we get that you went and talked to Pope," Lew said, impatient.

"Yeah, what did he say?"

"Well, better than you listening to me, you can listen to him," I said. I pressed the button on my phone and like magic Mister Pope's voice sounded in the conference room. Everyone leaned close to hear his words.

"Well, the main reason that none of the bird watching community has gotten involved in the whole lost bird thing, other than documenting it, is that by definition we are bird watchers. We are not supposed to interfere with the birds. We are simply watching them."

"I don't want to listen to this man talking about birds," Paris said, in an instant bored.

"Okay, I won't bore y'all with the conversation," I said pressing the button and stopping the recording. "All I will tell you is that Mister Pope pointed out that what we have to consider is that the bird we are going to rescue has been seen as far south as the Farrallon Islands and as far north as Devil's Slide. So, that is our target range. We have to determine where the best place to try and take him.

"Mister Pope pointed out that when Mo is in the Bay Area he likes flying to Alcatraz. He pointed out that Alcatraz is a national park. We can't grab Mo there even if he was next to us. We would be breaking government law. The punishments would be extreme."

I paused. I studied the others in the room. Rome was listening intently. Lew was taking notes. Seeing Lew scribbling down notes made me smile. Dre was listening as were most in the room. The only ones bored seemed to be Tanza, Paris and Cash. Cue, of course, was filming and stalking the conference room and trying to find the best angle for this camera to take in everyone.

"So, Mister Pope pointed out that we have to catch Mo and make sure he doesn't open his wings. If he opens his wings and they get, what did he say, catawampus, then we might as well kill Mo."

"Kill him?"

"Yeah, Mister Pope said that a bird that can't fly is dead anyway. So, we have to catch Mo and make sure it never opens its wings," I said.

"What about shooting it with a tranquilizer? You know, like in those animal shows?"

I shook my head. "I asked him that same question. He said tranquilizers are for mammals. Tranquilizers work based on weight. Birds look bigger than they are, but they are mostly feathers. Shooting Mo with a tranquilizer we're more likely to kill it than tranquilize it."

"How do we capture it?"

"Here's the hard part," I said. "We have to find it. We know it likes cliffsides. So, we go to one of those cliffsides and we get someone to rappel down off the cliff and swing to Mo. If Mo sees you coming it will fly off."

"Damn," Lew said.

"Yeah, but Mister Pope said it can be done. He participated in a hawk banding, where they put those leg bands on birds. So, whoever is crazy enough to rappel down and swing and catch Mo has to make sure that Mo doesn't open his wings. Here's the tricky part. Someone has to put Mo in a PVC pipe, avoiding the beak that is like a blunt spear. Mister Pope suggested wearing hockey pads to protect whoever goes from having their heart pierced. He also suggested wearing a hockey mask and goggles. Guaranteed Mo will not be interested in being captured. It will be completely freaked out. So, it will fight. If we can get it in the PVC pipe then it will calm down, until we push it out the other end."

"Geez," Derricka said.

"Yeah, Mister Pope said that is the easy part," I said. Everyone at the meeting looked at me disbelieving. "I think he was kidding. He has a weird sense of humor."

"Okay, say we get that far," Faith said, from the other side of the table. Her notebook was open, and she was taking notes like Dre. "What's next?"

"Mister Pope said that after capturing Mo and getting back up and off the cliff we would have to get the bird from California to Maine or Nova Scotia."

"Okay," Faith said looking at Cash. Cash nodded.

"Here's the tricky part," I said. "We have to get this bird to the east coast. We can't take a commercial plane. They aren't going to allow us to carry onboard a live animal. So, the only way we get Mo to the east coast is a private plane. But that ain't the tricky part. We have to travel, at the minimum, eight hours and Mister Pope had no idea how long the bird could survive without food."

"It's not going to eat?"

"Of course not," Tanza said. "It's all freaked out and stressed."

"So, Mister Pope decided the only way to make sure that Mo survives the flight is that we get a vet whose only job is to make sure that the bird is safe and healthy."

"Damn," Faith said.

"I know," I said. "I think we need to know the hurdles to make this happen."

"Yeah, you're right," Tanza said. "Is there anything else?"

"Well, the last twist is that we need to land in Nova Scotia, but that is Canada. So, that is all of a sudden an international issue.

We land. We trek Mo to the cliff side. We release him. He sees other birds that look like him. End of story."

"Damn," Dre said.

"Yeah," I said and chuckled. It was a relief to get it all off my shoulders. In unburdening myself the weight was straight away equally distributed to all the Rescuers.

There was quiet in the conference room. Rome shook his head. Lew pouted and looked at the notes Dre had taken. Derricka was busy taking pictures and posting them online. She had promised not to tell anyone online of the project until we either were successful or failed. The same promise had been made by Cue. Cash sat bored and was the first to speak.

"The way I see this we need at least four more people to make this happen. Two, at least, to swing and catch the bird. A vet. Where do we find a vet to sign off on this craziness and a pilot. I think that we may need to hire a lawyer in California and Maine and Nova Scotia to represent us, just in case. There are a lot of laws we will be breaking just to save some bird that doesn't want saving," Cash paused and added, "When do you think we are doing this?"

"I figure the best time would be next summer, maybe a week after school lets out," I said.

Cash nodded and pulled out his phone and started texting for the next five minutes nonstop.

"Okay, we have some work to do," Faith said. She gave everyone a job to complete before the next meeting. We were all asked to find some daredevils interested in rappelling down a cliff and capturing a bird that could pierce their heart or poke out their eyes. Faith, Dre and Tanza said they might know someone who could put them in contact with a veterinarian.

Before the meeting broke up Cash smiled and put his phone away.

"I got a lead on a private plane."

Cash had his moment.

We made plans for the summer of the end of our sophomore year and the beginning of our junior year. It was a really crazy projection. We were thinking a year in advance.

Everything was focused on the first week of June, a year from our next meeting.

We had two meetings in April, after Spring break. There was all this preparation for tests and closing of the school year in April.

At our fourth meeting Daniel Brewer and Michael Carson showed up for the first daredevil meeting. They had been invited by Derricka. Daniel was a bit of a daredevil and an attention seeker. He was a skateboarder and into extreme sports.

"Hey, Derricka invited me to this meeting to see if I could help you with my incredible climbing skills." Daniel Brewer had a cast on his left wrist that first meeting.

"What happened to your wrist?"

"I broke it trying to do a 360º Fakey Twist Flip," Daniel grinned, showing he had a missing tooth.

Michael Carson was this small shouldered unassuming type of character with a Milk dud shaped head. He was shorter than Daniel and most everyone in the lunchroom, where we met. He looked like a human weasel. His eyes were shifty. They never stopped flitting left to right while he was at the meeting.

"I don't think that I'm a fit for your little group," Carson said and unceremoniously walked out of the meeting.

Richie Hill showed up and seeing Daniel Brewster and Michael Carson sitting at the table shook his head and walked away.

Allen Lattimore was invited by Dre. They knew each other from church. Allen Lattimore was a slender kid who looked like he might be more comfortable out of doors than in. He had intense eyes and ears that seemed to desire to be wings. Lattimore showed up for the first meeting as well. He was a quiet fighter. It seemed most of the daredevils fought about one thing or another.

"The daredevils of the school are the bad boys of the school. They are not the nicest bunch. They are all trying to outdo each other. I can't imagine any of them working with each other unless they been doing things together," Lattimore said.

"What? Why?"

"They just don't trust each other. No one will work with Brewer because he's a bit of a wild man," Lattimore said.

"What about you," Lew asked.

"Me? I'm a little different. I will work with others as long as they aren't lunatics trying only to get likes. I like the physical challenges."

As Lattimore was talking Cash walked in with the daredevil brothers Jayden and Kayden Smith.

"These my guys," Cash grinned. "They the best."

Everyone knew the Smith brothers. They were infamous at Gee Dub. They were the first to climb on the roof of Gee Dub and get suspended. They had returned to school and been found on the roof of the gymnasium and been suspended. After the second suspension they were threatened with expulsion if they had any other infractions on school grounds.

The Smiths took their act on the road. They zip lined across Lake Merritt and were nearly arrested for the stunt. Their biggest stunt was climbing the side of the Kaiser building without any ropes. Of the daredevils at Gee Dub the Smiths were rock stars.

"Cash told us about the stunt. We're interested," Jayden said.

"My bro has the softest hands," Kayden Smith smiled.

"I think I like the element of danger in the stunt. We could go viral if we catch this beast."

"Man, we are one hundred percent in, if you want us," Kayden said.

After the daredevils came through, we voted on them. They were integral to the mission. We had to be all one hundred percent behind whoever we picked.

The last month of school at Gee Dub ended quietly. We had decided on our daredevils and had invited them to our first dry run. The Smith brothers were unavailable due to previous commitments with their family. They promised when they returned, they would be ready to participate in every aspect of the plan.

Chapter 16.

Summer

The last week of May was the last week of school my sophomore year. It was a good time. We had accomplished so much. But we were still looking for a veterinarian. Faith told me we would find one, meaning she and Tanza were looking.

Lew, Dre and Rome had notched their twentieth scholarships. We had assembled a group to rescue a lost bird. Things seemed to be moving along swimmingly.

Then we did our dry run. The Rescuers seemed a good name. Yet, the question was simply were we saving the lost bird or was it saving us?

Two weeks after school let out the Rescuers had driven to San Mateo in Rome's Lincoln Navigator. The day of the dry run Rome seemed a little nervous. It was a little surprising.

The drive down the 880 freeway was uneventful. Derricka was sitting in the passenger seat dressed in jeans, sweater and braids. Rome was being talkative. I was sitting two rows back next to Allen Lattimore and Faith studying the information about Devil's Slide but simultaneously hearing Rome laughing. Lew and Dre on the second row of the Navigator looked at each other. Rome was never that talkative.

Tanza and Cash sitting with Lew and Dre were too busy to notice Rome's over exuberance. Yet, I could not take my eyes off Rome. He was eating something from a bag. He popped a gummy into his mouth, and he reached for another gummy and tried to repeat the deft action. The gummy missed his mouth and gone flying in the front of the Navigator somewhere.

Rome, for an instant, looked down and tried to retrieve the gummy and nearly caused the Navigator to change lanes and kill everyone. He reacted and swerved and threw everyone in the SUV to the right and then the left as he corrected his oversteering. The reaction in the SUV was immediate.

"Are you mental," screamed Tanza. She was in the rear passenger seat next to Cash. Cash had fallen in between the seats, not wearing his seatbelt. In the third row of the Navigator, Allen, Faith and I held on with all our might as Rome regained control.

"Calm down," Rome screamed.

Rome was trying to impress Derricka, I thought. Paris was screaming like she was on fire. It had gone from calm and cool to one hundred percent chaos and madness.

"Auggie, you better do something," Faith screamed at me. What did she want me to do? I mean, I was sitting in the back of the Navigator with her thinking about a weekend at Devil's Slide waiting to see a bird which was not supposed to be on the West Coast. I was thinking of bigger things than Rome trying to impress Derricka and being a maniac. Paris was acting like she was having a heart attack and grabbing on me like I was a defibrillator.

"Auggie, tell him something," Paris snapped.

I looked at the girl who was two hundred percent attitude and was about to have it, when Faith pulled my arm and got my attention. I wanted to scream at Paris. I hated when people screamed at me. It was the one thing which drove me bonkers.

"Auggie, say something to him," Faith yelled over the yelling in the raucous Lincoln.

I looked at the round face with the apple cheeks behind the cat eyed sunglasses and paused. I took a deep breath and found myself not as angry. I looked from Faith to Paris to Tanza Smith, the banker, acting like she had nearly died. I shook my head and leaned forward, past Cash, the hookup, Lew and Dre and shouted at Rome, the driver, my best friend.

"Rome," I barked over everyone and for some unexplained reason everyone quieted. "Can you calm down and get us to Devil's Slide without killing us? We just need to get there in one piece. No drama."

In the quiet of the interior of the Navigator there was eerie silence.

From the driver's seat Rome nodded, cowed.

"Sorry," Rome said.

I leaned back and looked to Tanza and she smiled, satisfied. I smirked at the daughter of one of the biggest local rappers on the West Coast. I helped Cash up from between the seats and gave Paris my best don't-ever-scream-at-me-like-that-again looks before sitting back in my seat. Faith smiled at me and though I wanted to smile back I just gave her one last look and shook my head. That was all I could do. I wasn't driving. I didn't even have a license.

I knew no one wanted Rome to drive but he was the son of the father who had given him the Lincoln Navigator. Thankfully, Rome only nearly killed us once before we got to the park. He exited the freeway and drove us to the parking lot.

"Rescuers we have arrived," Rome smiled, parking the Navigator near a dumpster.

"Screw you very much," Tanza Smith said, climbing out of the Navigator still steamed at Rome.

"Hey, chill," Cash said. Tanza rolled her eyes and headed to the rear of the Navigator to get her bag.

Derricka Monroe, the youngest of the Rescuers, adjusted her backpack and scanned the parking lot. There were only a handful of cars parked in the lot.

"This is perfect," Derricka smiled, showing off her dimples as she adjusted her overstuffed backpack on her small shoulders. "We shouldn't have anyone near us while we look for the best way to catch the uncatchable."

By the time I had climbed out Faith and Rome were slowly making their way to the rear of the Navigator and fetching their bags. Everyone had a backpack and a tent or camping supplies. I grabbed my sleeping bag and Rome stood and looked like a lost puppy.

"What man?" I said, all of a sudden annoyed. "Say something."

"I'm sorry, I nearly killed everyone," Rome whispered.

"It's no big deal. You didn't kill us. We're here," I said, realizing Rome was sorry.

Paris shouldered past us and gave Rome a death stare. Tanza followed, ever the drama queen. Faith was close behind.

"Screw you, Jerome," Tanza spat. "That was some stupid low grade ship breaking stuff."

"It's okay, Rome," Cue smiled. "We ain't dead."

"Yeah, it's cool. Long as you don't do nothing so stupid again," Lew laughed.

"Yeah, and you probably got Derricka all thinking you're a bad boy," Cash giggled.

We moved to the rear of the Navigator and divvied up the equipment and supplies.

"Okay, now that we are all feeling better, let's head to the campsite," Faith grinned, and the Rescuers headed to the trail which led to the San Pedro Valley Park.

"We got a three-mile hike," Derricka announced as Rome began to walk.

The brawn of the crew, Rome Ward, had been all gung-ho for the three-mile walk to Devil's Slide. He was the designated schlepper of equipment. The strategist, Faith Henry had plotted the possible location of the treasure. She and Paris booked our campsite. Tanza made sure we brought the right equipment.

The videographer, Cue, had all sorts of video equipment in a rucksack. He also was prepared for anything. In his backpack he showed me he had bear spray, even though there had not been a bear sighting in over two hundred years.

The diplomat, tasked with getting whatever was needed, Cash, thought himself a camper and liked the idea of camping out for the weekend. The person bank rolling the whole operation, Tanza Smith was complaining constantly and being an annoyance whenever she opened her mouth. Dre, the long-range travel planner, had decided to be the Sherpa for Tanza Smith. He took her bags and his to the campsite.

"We should get to the campsite in under an hour," Rome announced. "We should have plenty of time to set up camp before nightfall."

When we arrived at the campsite, we only had a couple of hours before nightfall. So, we pitched camp and our tents and made our dinner and first night's schedule.

We ate a bunch of fast food and afterwards, with flashlights walked around the campsite and listened to the night. There wasn't too much to do on Devil's Slide if you were a teenager or a person with half a brain. For us though, it was the night which held the greatest possibilities.

A little after sunset we prepared for our night's excursion.

"Remember, we are going to be near a cliff at night," I said. "If there is any accident everyone go to plan B. Sacrifice for the good of the majority."

"Auggie, you know there is no reason for us to have a plan B," Cue said, clicking on his infrared camera. "We are just trying to find where a bird sleeps. It's not like we are looking for Big Foot."

"Never can be too careful," I said.

The ten of us trekked to the cliffside and scanned the rocky ledges for Mo.

"Think we need to separate," I said.

"No, man, that's exactly what they say in every horror movie ever made, the minute before someone comes up missing," Rome said.

"This ain't a horror movie," Tanza pointed out. She hooked her arm in Cash's and moved up the cliffside. Rome and Derricka went in another direction. Paris, Allen and Dre went in another direction. Lew and Cue followed behind Rome and Derricka. That left me and Faith.

"I guess it's you and me," Faith said.

"Okay, be careful," I said, "I don't want to have to save your life."

We walked up and down the cliffside and after a few minutes I received a text message from Lew. Faith looked at her phone at the same time.

"They found it," I said.

We walked and found Cue and Lew by a tree. **All the Rescuers were lined along the cliff's edge looking at Mo.** They were looking down the edge of the cliff toward a low lip maybe fifty feet below their feet. I, for an instant, tried to move to the cliff's edge but frightened, feeling the darkness pulling me forward, I reversed and bumped into Faith.

"Auggie, you okay?"

Lew turned and caught me as I ricocheted off Faith and moved dizzily toward the cliff's edge.

"Auggie, relax," Lew said grabbing me by my wrist.

I must have blacked out for a minute. All I remember is I was seated on the ground with my back against a tree. Faith and Tanza were watching me like I was about to hand them a bag of money.

"What's wrong with you?"

"Nothing," I said, a little embarrassed.

"He doesn't do well with heights," Lew said.

I tried to climb to my feet and Lew and Faith helped me up.

"I'm fine."

"You need to not be all crazy if you can't stand heights, Auggie," Faith said, a little concern in her voice.

After returning to the camp in the darkness we watched as Rome and Cash failing at starting a fire.

"How can you not be able to make a fire? I mean, cavemen made fires," Paris laughed.

"Well, you are more than welcome to try your hand at this," Rome said.

Cash handed his sticks to Dre and Dre passed them to Allen.

"Allen might be able to do something with this," Faith said, with a smile. "He is a daredevil."

In a few minutes Allen had a fire started. Of course, as soon as the fire got going Rome and Cash were trying to put tree trunks on the flame. They were a little excited by the idea of fire.

The Rescuers sat and ate what passed as our dinner of hotdogs, baked beans, marshmallows and soda. Lew reminded everyone to throw their trash in the bag he had, and he would put it in the locked trashbin.

"We can't have wildcats or coyotes prowling and looking for food. They have a keen sense of smell."

We sat in a circle around the campfire for a few hours and talked about nothing important. It was a nice moment. Faith, in the natural glow of the firelight, looked like someone different. Paris, Derricka and Tanza too, away from Gee Dub, and framed against the night sky, took on celestial qualities.

We roasted marshmallows and laughed and talked about the rescue. The dry run had, so far, been incredibly successful. Now, we just had to hope that in twelve months that Mo survived, and we managed to keep our group together to see the bird captured and returned to its kind.

Derricka was the first to head to the girl's tent. She was followed by Paris and Faith and finally Tanza. Lew, the fire manager, let the fire die down. He was the last to move to our tent as the darkness took hold of the campsite.

The tents were on the far side of the camp with the firepit in the middle. The bathrooms and trash were on the other side of camp.

We were all safely in our tent, but no one seemed really sleepy. It was still relatively early, so we all sat in our tents and talked for a while.

"You think it moves around a lot at night?"

"I can't imagine it would. I mean, it's on a cliff. Not too much bothers it up there."

There was quiet.

"You think there are any bears out here?"

"We're in San Mateo," Cash announced. "The closest thing to bears are Shriners or Kiwanis. You ask me."

"The thing we might see are raccoons, bobcats or coyotes," Derricka said.

"Great," Tanza breathed. "I hate coyotes."

"Nobody likes coyotes," Faith said. The four girls were all in one tent. They had sleeping bags and all sorts of things to keep them entertained. Faith had her phone and a power bank for the overnight excursion. The power bank had ten hours of power, supposedly.

"Why didn't we come here just at night and leave once we found the bird?"

"Well, we had to walk three miles just to get here," Allen pointed out.

"I think walking back in the dark with all the animals all around would not be a good thing," Lew said.

"Yeah, the girls wo-wo-would freak out," Dre said.

"We would spend more time protecting them than getting out," Rome said.

"Yeah, we can leave in the morning with all the information we need," Cash smiled.

"Yeah, we don't want to scare the girls," I said, with a smile.

We got quiet. Dre turned on his little Bluetooth speaker and connected it to his phone. We listened to music until Dre's cell phone battery started to die.

Allen Lattimore had a power bank, but it was not working correctly. We spent about thirty minutes trying to solve the energy problem and recharge Dre's phone. Rome had brought two battery-operated lanterns and gave one to the girls. He let the lantern burn down before we got quiet. In the lull, I tried to think of what was next.

Allen and Dre got the power bank to charge Dre's phone enough before we all started to get sleepy. Rome began to doze. Cash got quiet. I yawned. In the quiet of the tent my eyelids got heavy.

"Hey, Auggie," Dre said before I began to doze.

"Yeah," I asked.

"Can you walk with me to the toilet?"

I smiled.

"Yeah, sure," I unzipped my sleeping bag and heard Dre unzip his as well.

"Hey, wait for me," said Cash in the tent's darkness. "I may as well go, since you guys are going."

By the time I found my flashlight and Dre found his flashlight everyone in the tent was doing a Soul Train line to the toilet.

We walked past the smoldering fire, just embers and ash really. The toilet was maybe one hundred yards from the campsite. In the darkness though, it seemed like miles.

I looked up and smiled. **The stars were out and brilliant.** The stars seemed to be just inches from my outstretched fingers.

As Allen Lattimore, Rome, Lew, Dre, Cash, Cue and I moved quietly toward the toilet we heard noises in the darkness. Every noise got us throwing the beams of light from our flashlights in the direction of the sound.

"This is ridiculous," Rome announced and tried to walk forward in the darkness. As he marched forward there was a noise to the left of the group.

"What was that?"

"Man, let's hurry up and get to the toilet," Lew said. "I ain't built for camping."

"You?"

"Man, ain't none of us built for this."

"Hey, Rome, what do you think if we hoof it down to the Navi and sleep there?"

The toilet was on the far side of the campsite. We had been smart to not camp next to the trash or the bathroom. Lew had warned us that the animals loved prowling by the locked trash bin. They were curious about the toilets as well.

"Someone stand guard. If anything comes call out," Rome said as he walked into the toilet first. Cash followed Rome. After Cash was Cue. Allen Lattimore was next. Lew followed Lattimore. Dre was the second to last. I was the last in the toilet.

When I came out, I found Lew and Dre standing guard.

"Thanks for waiting."

"Of course," Lew said.

"Where's Rome?"

Just then Rome snuck from behind and grabbed me.

I must have jumped ten feet in the air.

Lew and Dre fell out. Rome hit the ground and was laughing as if scaring me was the funniest thing on earth. I had tossed my flashlight when Rome scared me and spun around and pretended to look for it.

"Man, did you see his face?"

Dre made a scared expression.

"Naw, man, he was more like this," Lew said, twisting his face up like he had eaten a worm.

"That was worth all the guff I got getting us here," Rome laughed.

I found my flashlight. I clicked the button and the light blinked on and then off. I clicked it again and discovered my light was dead.

"What's wrong?"

"My flashlight stopped working," I said.

"It wasn't made to be thrown into the dark, I suppose," Rome said, with a smile.

"Don't worry about it," Lew said. "We just heading back to the tent. Ain't nothing out here to worry about, except Rome scaring you."

I shook my head.

The crew, the originals, walked back toward the camp. They flashed their lights to the left and right as we walked. Rome was ahead of me. I was trailing, taking up the rear.

We were near the firepit when Lew stopped and flashed his light to the right. Dre stopped just behind Lew and shined his light in the same direction.

"What you see?"

"I'm not sure," Lew said, under his breath. "I think there's something out there though."

Rome threw his beam of light in the same direction as Lew and Dre and I tried to see what they were doing. I thought Rome was trying to scare me again. So, I did not really pay attention.

In the darkness there were a pair of red eyes looking back at us from the trees. The eyes were low to the ground, maybe two or three feet high and ten or twenty feet away.

"What is that?"

"I don't know and I ain't going to stay to find out," Lew said and spun and bumped into Dre. Dre stepped back and bounced off Rome. Rome fell on his butt but managed to hit me in so doing. Instantaneously, Lew and Dre were moving back as fast as they could away from the red eyes and Rome was trying to scramble to his feet.

Being last I nearly avoided the chaos and madness of the crew's panic. Rome pushed me and the shove was so unexpected I tripped and fell. I landed awkwardly and rolled over and scrambled to my feet and ran with my friends the rest of the way to the tents.

When we made it to the tents Lew and Dre laughed and shook their heads at Rome falling on his ass.

"You saw him go down like when Cap mopped Iron Man," Lew asked, smiling from ear-to-ear.

Rome shook his head.

We climbed back into the tent. We slipped into our sleeping bags. The tent quieted.

"I'm glad we only have to do this once," Rome said.

"We might need to do this one more time, to be sure," I said. "We need to make sure the bird sleeps in the same place."

"Great," said Rome.

"The bird ain't going to save itself," I said.

Rome rolled his eyes.

Chapter 17.

August-January

My junior year at Gee Dub was always determined by my schedule. Like every year I had Advisory first period of the day. Mister Pope was my advisory teacher again. I liked the consistency. I knew what to expect from Pope. English was the second class of the day with Miss Maxine Timmons. I liked English but I had heard horror stories about Miss Timmons. She was brilliant but slow to get your work back. Last year, Shelia Miller complained to Mister Allen about not getting her work back for a full marking period. I hoped things were going to be better than that. I figured if there was no work coming back, I would go to Allen or Davenport or Mister Pope and tell them it was stressing me out. Of course, school hadn't begun, and I was already seeing problems.

I took a deep breath and skimmed the remainder of my schedule. Art was third with Mister Cheeks. I liked Cheeks. He was an artist. I mean a real artist. He had a few art pieces in a gallery in San Francisco. He was a visual artist and focused on bigger concepts I did not understand.

PE was fourth period and right before lunch. I liked PE. I know I wasn't supposed to like it, but I liked running around and learning about sports everyone loved for some reason. After lunch I had Math with Mister Hampton. Spanish 3 was on my schedule as my sixth period with Señor Owen. Owen was okay. He was one of the few non-black staff members of Gee Dub. I remember Mister Boyd, my Spanish 2 teacher, telling me he and Mister Owen went to Mexico for a week and had a blast.

My Science class was taught by Miss Oliver. I didn't know anything about Miss Oliver. She was new in Gee Dub. Question mark. Need to feel her out. Hoped she was a good teacher and not easily derailed.

The last class of the day was a two-year jag which led to Gee Dub's Senior project. The junior year or the first half of the Senior project was begun in US Government with the legendary Mister Lancaster. In US Government class all juniors were given their first group project to be publicly critiqued. Lancaster taught two years of US Government. He switched off with another legend at Gee Dub, Doctor Bryant. So, while Lancaster taught US Government to juniors, Doctor Bryant taught US History and Policy to Seniors.

My junior year was the first year I would have to do mandated group projects.

The beginning of school was always hectic. There were all these teachers and the teacher's personalities to get used to, while negotiating the fragile dynamics of school politics daily in Gee Dub. My personal haters club was still active and recruiting members.

Mercedes Copeland, my crush from my freshman year, was dating a senior now who played on the football team. I saw her every so often, but my junior year I had no classes with the girl who had stolen my heart and nearly destroyed my friendships as a result.

"What's up Auggie," Lew said as I entered the lunchroom after PE. Everyone was now at the junior table, everyone now included Faith and Cash, Tanza and Derricka. I smiled seeing the Rescuers all at the same table.

We all exchanged our schedules and made note of it if we had any classes together. Faith and I had Art together. Cash was in the same Science class. Everyone else was in different classes.

I worked and studied and went to the bi-weekly meetings for the Rescuers, but I was focused on my grades and scholarships and bringing the project we had worked for two years to a close.

The meetings were the beginning of the year just about equipment needed to catch the bird. For a long while we considered a net gun, but everyone thought it was too much of a high-risk item. Instead, the daredevils were going to have to sneak up on the bird and catch it by surprise. Cue filmed everything.

There were holes in the plan, but we had time to patch those holes.

By Thanksgiving break we were deciding on the diameters of the tubes for Mo. We had settled on the length but needed the diameter to be right. We had to have half a dozen of those PVC pipes, just in case we lost one or three to the cliff.

Rome was tasked with a running budget. Tanza and Cash insisted on it. Rome had laughed, understanding the reason was their parent's accountants wanted to write off everything for their taxes.

Rome was also supposed to check in on the daredevils. They were supposed to be figuring out a way to sneak up on Mo and catch it without harming it. Jayden and Kayden Smith were impressive. They were like circus performers. They seemed fearless. Allen Lattimore, always so calm and cool, had an ability to do some things physically which seemed impossible. He was an excellent par course enthusiast and incredible strong and fast. Allen and Kayden had the softest hands. For their rigs they insisted on rubber bands, no less than a dozen carabiners, rappelling gloves, Kevlar vests, and infrared goggles. The climbing ropes based on the descent were 9.5-9.9mm Non-Dry and Dry rope. Of course, all three were very particular to their rope of choice.

Lew focused on making everything eco-friendly. He and Paris were tasked with finding the best defense attorneys in California, Maine and Nova Scotia. They had written down all the laws which would be broken to take Mo from California to Nova Scotia. They then had documented all the laws which would be broken or bent taken Mo from California to Maine and then to Nova Scotia. The list of laws was daunting. Paris and Lew had to go through a huge list of defense attorneys and then research their record of getting people out of jail for state and federal infractions.

Dre and Derricka were given the job of finding protective equipment for the daredevils. Of course, the first place they went was the PE department. The Gee Dub PE department seemed to not know what hockey equipment was or consisted of and more importantly were not forthcoming with anything. D&D were stonewalled.

"What should we do," Derricka asked Tanza at a meeting.

Tanza, who was generally dry in her tone, was flaming when she responded, "Dee, this ain't that hard. You got a shopping list. You get on Google and find what you need. You buy it, if you balling. If not, then you bring the list to us. We ain't babysitting nobody. We get to it when we get to it. You and Dre got your duties. If you me, you figure out a workaround and get your stuff and keep your head down." She was no one to play with. "To be the boss you have to be willing to pay the cost."

With Tanza's guidance Derricka and Dre were working on getting the short list of items for the daredevils.

Cash had a plane ready at the San Francisco Airport to jet us from California to Nova Scotia starting the first of June. He also said we would have an Escalade to drive us to the Atlantic from the airport, whichever airport we landed at. Getting a SUV in Canada was complicated but doable.

Based on Faith and Tanza's calculations we would be gone for two days, at most, having no hiccups or trouble. If we released Mo, based on our plan, we should have been gone no more than nine hours, max. The goal was to find where gannets gathered and release Mo there. If we released him early enough, we could be back in California by dinner the next day. At least, that was the plan.

All these things were happening, and school swirled around us, simultaneously. The calendar just moved on. Days slid off the calendar and pushed us toward Thanksgiving and Christmas break.

The week before Thanksgiving break Lew was all smiles at the lunch table.

"I have submitted my twenty-fifth scholarship, Auggie," Lew admitted.

"Me, too," said Dre.

"I thought we were only going to submit twenty," Rome said, with a smile. "I submitted thirty. Now, I think this year and next the funds should start rolling in, if your information is correct, Auggie."

The Thanksgiving assembly flitted by and I was hard pressed to recall who performed my junior year. I was so focused on so many other things. There was a mammoth list of things to gather before June. My mind simply reeled at all the information being daily delivered to me to sort out and delegate.

Faith regularly kept me up to date on the weather and the latest information about Mo. She had over Thanksgiving found a website and camera devoted to the cliffs of Half Moon Bay. Every so often there were sightings of Mo.

When we returned to school in January Faith found me and told me we were meeting on the bleachers.

"Happy New Year to you," I smiled.

Faith rolled her eyes at my attempt to be cordial and walked away and disappeared in the sea of students heading to their classes.

In January, it seemed the junior teachers all came back on fire. They had clear deadlines for us. Thankfully, only three classes had ambitious projects laid out for us in January. Of course, there were the two big papers assigned for English. The first was due the week after Valentine's Day. The second paper was due the week after Spring break. There was an individual project for Science, student's choice and a group assignment for the same class dealing with an element of science which showed the most potential. All those group assignments were going to be entered into the Gee Dub science fair. The last and perhaps the most daunting was the US Government group project for Mister Lancaster. It was due a week after Spring break, like my last English paper. It was half of my grade in the last semester.

With all the information swimming in my head I walked out of US Government and headed to the football field. It was cool but not cold that day. By the time I reached the bleachers most of the Rescuers were seated and talking amongst themselves.

"We have five months to make all our hard work pay off," Faith said, standing next to Tanza. Tanza was dressed in a Canadian Goose down ski jacket. Her outfit screamed thousands of dollars without her saying a word. Her Burberry backpack sat between her shoulder blades as she stood wearing dark blue designer jeans and Coach boots.

I sat next to Dre and Allen and let Faith and Tanza catch everyone up. It was cool and a perfect place to have a meeting. Few people liked to go out when it was cold. That guaranteed privacy.

Cue was filming everything. He had one of those cameras which was almost like a TV camera but smaller. Cue was a sophomore but motivated. We told him that he would have to commit to documenting the entire project or we would not give him credit at the end.

Our failsafe videographer was Derricka. Tanza and Derricka were old friends. They were like me and Lew, Rome and Dre. She recommended her and said, if Cue failed, we could always count on Derricka. Like Tanza, Derricka was a social media content creator. She had a following of somewhere near 25k.

"Okay, here's the deal," Tanza began. "We have five months to go from plan to reality. We have a good group here. We just have to make sure that everyone does what they say they can."

I looked over the ten faces looking back at me and paused. In the crowd was the latest recruit Maya Wimberly. Faith had come through and found a girl who volunteered at the zoo. She was our in for a veterinarian. Faith gestured to me and Tanza poked out her lip as I climbed to my feet and climbed off the bleachers. I reluctantly spoke.

"In order to make this happen everyone has to be on board. If you are uncertain or unable to do your job, we need to know now. If things change, we need to know now. We are operating like this is one of those Mission Impossible movies. There are a lot of moving parts and a lot of money involved."

Tanza stepped forward and spoke, "Oh, yeah, before we get too far, I have NDAs for everyone to sign and get back to me. No one can jeopardize our chances to getting into college. No one." Tanza was an influencer on one of the social platforms. We had to make Tanza promise not to tip off anyone about what we were doing until June. She recruited Cue and Derricka and Cash. Tanza made everyone sign NDAs. Her father had advised her of that stipulation. Her father had a lawyer on retainer, and he advised Tanza through the project, since there was money involved.

Signing the non-disclosure agreement made the whole project real. It had been real before, but with the signature and threat of lawsuits things became increasingly concrete.

"Things just got real," Dre joked.

I could only shake my head at the Bad Boy reference.

Chapter 18.

February-June

I was trying to make sure everything was going smoothly. I didn't want to fail anyone, especially so close to the end. In my mind I had to make sure of all the things I was responsible for in the plan were completed. Faith and Tanza had given me the responsibility to manage the boys who were trying to prepare for capturing the wild bird on the cliffs. On its face, the job Faith and Tanza gave me seemed just like looking over someone's shoulder, but it was much more.

I checked in with each person every week. The ones I thought were going to be the easiest were the hardest. The ones I imagined were going to be a pain were a pain and a half. There were eight boys on the project. There was only three who did not give me grief and one of them was me.

Dre, although quiet was stubborn. He knew what he was doing and hated when people did not trust him to do his work. I found myself treating the talented Andre Potter like a diva. I couldn't ask too many questions. I couldn't come by too often.

Lew was no different. He wanted space to work. When Lew saw me, he frowned. "I didn't know that I would have to become an amateur lawyer to prepare for all the laws and regulations we are going to break, just going to Devil's Slide and then going to the airport."

"Well, you were always interested in the law," I admitted.

Rome was always moody and given the task of keeping up with the daredevils he was a mess. Talking to him was like juggling nitroglycerin. Anything could set him off.

Allen, Jayden and Kayden were busy being daredevils and working on having soft hands. They did not really need too much supervision, according to Rome.

The two easiest to deal with were surprisingly Cash and Cue. Of course, I imagined Cash to be a Primadonna, but he was smart, resourceful and reliable. His over-the-top clothing was a minor extravagance but nothing to concern myself about.

Cash, the transport man was the easiest to get along with. He was well connected. Any time I asked him about his assignment he was always chipper. All he had to do was make some calls. He had secured an airplane. I asked for a picture of the plane. I asked for details. Cash was more than willing to accommodate.

Cue was still one hundred percent committed and filming every meeting and taking the raw footage and trying to edit the footage and make it into a story.

Faith caught me in the hallway near my Math class. She was dressed in a white blouse and blue skirt. Her hair was in braids and somehow held up in a gravity defying style that looked a little like a mushroom and a little like a nest of finger thin snakes. Her big almond shaped eyes were smiling.

"What are you doing for Valentine's Day?" Faith asked.

"I think I'll be doing what I did last year for Valentines," I said. "Nothing."

Faith was looking at me with those big brown eyes. I was smiling and when I saw Faith looking at me, I fumbled.

"You want to go this year?"

"With you?" I asked.

I looked at Faith and for what seemed forever I noticed the girl in front of me was no longer the shapeless and unattractive person I had palled around with last year. Faith, the Faith I grew up with, had transformed into this incredibly attractive creature talking to me in the hallway.

"No strings attached, just going to the dance and dancing and then going home," Faith said behind those big brown eyes.

"Well, yeah," I smiled.

"Okay, I'll meet you there," Faith said.

"Okay," I said.

Faith spun around and walked away and into the retreating students heading to their classes. I watched her walk away and found myself smiling for an unknown reason.

A week before the Valentine's Day dance and I got a little antsy. I tried to dismiss it because of my general worry about my grades or my paper I was preparing to turn in or a hundred other things, but I knew it was because of Faith Henry.

The day before the dance everyone was sitting at the lunch table and I found myself looking at Faith on the other side of the table. She was wearing those finger thin braids in a loose ponytail. She was sitting with her back to me, her elbow on the table, her fist beneath her chin, listening to Tanza talk about something.

I shook the thought of Faith being anything but Faith. She was a girl I knew from Frederick Douglass. When I was in junior high school I didn't think about Faith or for that matter anyone other than my friends.

How had I suddenly found Faith Henry to be something other than the Faith of freshman and sophomore year? I looked at Dre and found him smiling and eating a piece of pizza. Lew was looking at his Science textbook on the table. Rome was joking with Allen Lattimore. No one seemed to notice my internal struggle, thankfully.

The dance was after school. I didn't go home. I just put my backpack in the locker and went to the gymnasium.

The Valentine's Day dance came in the middle of the month on a Thursday. The gym, for one night was transformed into a Cupid and cherubim heavy space. Pink and red streamers hung throughout the gymnasium. On the stage, in the back of the gym a DJ and his booth were set up. On the stage were theater speakers. The music began a little after school let out and played until ten o'clock that night.

I strolled in as casually as possible into the darkened gymnasium. There were strobe lights flashing and allowing students to see each other. I walked in the transformed gym and looked for Faith. There were easily forty or fifty people there already. About half were on the parquet dance floor. The basketball court was covered in rubber mats to protect the flooring below.

"Hey, Auggie," Paris said.

I looked at Paris and found her next to Tanza and beside Tanza stood the smiling Faith. Faith and Tanza and Paris were at the Valentine's Day dance. I was surprised. I thought only Faith would be there.

"You actually came?"

I looked at Tanza and did not answer her.

"How long you staying?"

"Don't know," I said to Tanza, the inquisitor. "How 'bout you?"

Tanza only smiled.

I looked around suddenly, wondering who else from the Rescuers was at the Valentine's Day dance. Out of the corner of my eye appeared Cash. He sauntered toward our small little group. I looked around for anyone else I might have missed. No one else from the Rescuers seemed to be at the dance.

"What's up, Auggie," Cash said, and we exchanged a dap and hand slap.

I opened my mouth only to close it. Nothing I was going to say that moment mattered.

The music changed and the girls seemed to suddenly want to dance. Tanza grabbed Cash and they walked out to the parquet dance floor. Paris looked around and found Wayne something, an average looking boy who I had seen every day but never gotten to know, standing near the dance floor and grabbed him by his arm and dragged the stunned boy toward the dance floor.

I smiled. I watched Tanza and Cash dancing. I also watched Paris and Wayne whatever next to Tanza and Cash. Tanza and Paris waved to Faith. I swallowed and tried to screw up the courage to ask Faith to dance.

"You want to dance?" I finally blurted out.

"Sure," Faith smiled.

I reached out my hand and Faith took it. We walked to the dance floor. We stepped onto the parquet floor which had been set up for the dance and Faith seemed to bounce and float on the dance floor. I smiled. I couldn't help it. Seeing Faith dancing made me smile.

I danced and laughed and smiled as Cash and Tanza gyrated near us. Paris and Wayne danced, but it was really just Paris dancing and spinning around with Tanza and Faith. Cash and I danced by each other and watched as the girls seemed just glad to be together in the strobe lights and music. It was a nice feeling. I enjoyed the distraction from the business of Gee Dub, grades, homework, scholarships and our plan to rescue Mo.

We danced for a few songs. In the cafeteria there were light refreshments. We ate and around eight thirty we left the cafeteria and headed back to the dance floor. By nine thirty we were laughing and talking in the parking lot. Cash offered to give me a ride home.

"Did you have fun?" Paris asked.

I nodded.

There were several cars parked in the lot. We stood in the front of the school waiting. Cash and Tanza were standing close to one another. Paris and Faith were talking.

The two girls came and sandwiched me. I felt a little uncomfortable. Paris smiled like she knew something I didn't. Faith smiled too.

"Auggie, I have to say I didn't know you had dance moves," Paris said.

I smiled, a little embarrassed.

"Yeah, I was surprised," Faith smiled.

"I kind of thought you were a stiff, but you had some moves," Tanza laughed still beside Cash.

At that moment a new black Range Rover appeared. It slid around the parked cars to the front of the school. Behind the Range Rover followed a silver Porsche SUV.

"That's us," Faith said as Tanza gave Cash a peck on the cheek and climbed into the rear of the Range Rover followed by Paris.

"Thanks for inviting me," I said to Faith.

"Sure," Faith said. I awkwardly hugged Faith and we neither found the moment to do anything but be awkward before I released her, and she climbed into the Range Rover.

The Porsche SUV passenger door opened and out stepped a man who was dressed in a black suit, white collared shirt and black tie.

The man opened the back door and watched as Cash climbed in the SUV. I climbed in behind Cash.

"Where to?"

I gave my address to the driver. I looked at Cash and back at the driver as the man who looked like he was CIA climbed into the SUV.

"Cash, that your dad," I asked as we sat in the rear of the Porsche SUV. The man behind the wheel looked a little like Cash, in that he was brown, he had thick eyebrows and full lips. The second man, dressed like a Secret Service agent, had a high forehead, broad nose, an earring in his left ear lobe and a trimmed goatee.

"Naw, my dad is in Europe right now," Cash said. "He's in a movie or doing a song for a movie or something." Cash sat back in the comfort of the SUV. "These are the guys my dad pays to make sure I'm safe."

"Safe?"

"Yeah, the ugly side of being the son of someone famous," Cash said.

I nodded. Cash tapped a few buttons and on the back of the headrest's videos blinked on.

"You got a favorite movie you want to watch?"

I shrugged.

"You want to see my dad's latest video?"

I couldn't say no. Cash was giving me a ride home. We sat back and watched videos as the driver drove me home.

"Thanks," I said as I climbed out of the SUV.

"Sure," Cash smiled as the Porsche SUV drove into the night.

The next day school soldiered on. Lew, Rome and Dre sat at the lunch table and joked and kidded about some boy who got in trouble in Math class.

"Security had to come," Lew said. "It was a mess."

Faith sat at the lunch table next to Paris and Tanza and they laughed and talked and said hey, but nothing significant. Cash sat at my elbow and smiled.

"What's up Cash?"

"Nothing, just checking in on you," Cash said.

I nodded.

The Black History month celebration was great as it always was as the students performed their hearts out. In that assembly Rome sang. Beyond Rome's performance I could not name any acts or students that performed. That same month I turned in my first of three papers for English. I wrote on the mental struggle of the Invisible Man in Ralph Ellison's novel.

In a blink of an eye, we were in March. Three months to go before we made all the work a reality.

I began reading several books about the industrial prison system and almost immediately knew what my second paper for English class was going to focus on.

As we sped through March, I prepared to compose my second essay for English. While I was gathering my thoughts for my English paper Cash and I decided to work together on our Science project. He just walked up to me and said, "Auggie, we already are working together out of school. We might as well work together on this Science project."

On the surface it seemed logical, but once I began working with Cash, I realized that he was completely the opposite of me. He was a slacker. He was spoiled. He was lazy. His work ethic was nearly nonexistent. I could not understand how he got good grades at Gee Dub.

"What did you do your individual project on," I asked.

"I can't remember, something about molecules and atoms, I think," Cash smiled.

I was stymied by his answer.

"You know that you work way too hard to get good grades, Auggie," Cash said.

"What you mean?"

"I mean, you are an overachiever. I have seen them before. You smell like you like to work hard."

I wasn't sure if I was supposed to be insulted by his comment.

"See, this is just dress rehearsal," Cash said. "The stuff they are teaching us is just to see if we can listen, learn and are willing to learn."

"And," I said, impatiently.

"And, the trick is to know what they are focusing on. This is four years of a job interview," Cash said.

I didn't agree with Cash. That was not surprising. What was surprising was how Cash approached the Science project. He was one of those kids who was always trying to look around the corner to find the shortcut.

He came to me one day and said that Missus Oliver was reading a copy of Scientific American. He pulled the very same copy out of his backpack. She was really interested in nanotubes, Cash noted.

"What are nanotubes?"

"Beats me, but I bet if we do a little research on nanotubes, we get a good grade on our project."

I had not found a scientific theory or practice as of yet and tried Cash's theory. We did the research and I found nanotubes to be very interesting. Cash only cared Missus Oliver was going to be over the moon seeing a pair of her students interested in something she was interested in.

"I guarantee she gives us a good grade."

It felt like cheating though we were not cheating. We were doing the research. We were learning about something scientific and that was what Missus Oliver wanted us to do.

At the same time as I was working on the group Science project, I was working on my group project for US Government. Mister Lancaster was a no-nonsense teacher who had an incredible classroom presence. He was six-foot-seven-inches tall and the color of sand with wavy black hair which fell just below his big ears. Lancaster was this incredibly gigantic figure with similarly gigantic features. His hands and fingers seemed to be the size of two regular human hands and fingers. His index finger seemed to stretch forever when he pointed. He had bluish brown eyes and depending on the light his eyes flashed blue or brown. He was angular and possessed high cheekbones and a slightly hooked nose.

Upon starting the school year Lancaster addressed the dozen questions he knew students needed to know about him.

"I have always been big. When I was in sixth grade, I was nearly six-foot tall. By the time I hit high school I was six-foot-five inches tall. I played basketball in high school. I got a scholarship. Went to college in New York. Studied History. Loved History. Got married. My wife and I moved to Los Angeles. I got my teaching credential. Things fell apart. She moved back to New York. I moved to Oakland. I started working here."

Mister Lancaster was a great teacher. He laid the information before us and allowed us to figure things out. He never spoon-fed us. I liked that.

So, when we were given the parameters of our group assignment I hesitated. I dreaded group assignments. They, in my brief history of schooling, were always abysmal. I usually did all the work, and my partner got half the credit. In US Government though it did not happen that way. I had been partnered with a strangely bright character who liked to be called: Chance. His real name was Chauncey Harper.

Spring break was approaching when Chauncey sat down and talked with me about the US Government topic. I found myself arguing with Chauncey at first about the Constitution, the Bill of Rights and finally voting rights. Chauncey eloquently destroyed my argument on the Constitution.

"I would love to write about the flaws of the Constitution and the fallacy of voting rights, but I don't think we have enough time to discuss either fully," Harper noted.

We instead decided to work on the rewriting of the ten essential amendments of the Bill of Rights. It was Chauncey's idea.

"The way I see it, the biggest problem in the US Government is the Bill of Rights," Chauncey reiterated. "Simply because they are the lies by which we falsely believe everything in being a private citizen resides." He continued, "We aren't given the same rights as everyone else. We aren't protected. We aren't included in the we of We the People."

"How so?"

"The Constitution, the Bill of Rights, all of it, in a way, is a fallacy by exclusion," Chauncey decided. "We were never considered in the writing." He paused. "We were considered in the drafting because Jefferson and his ilk bedded our ancestors and knew them not as one third of a human, but we were never meant to be considered to have the same rights as the citizens of this blood bought nation. Thus, we need to rewrite it to include us."

I listened. I thought about what Chauncey said and beside his desire to be called Chance his reasoning was sound. We agreed. He took the first five amendments. I took the last five amendments and created a Bill of Rights to represent everyone in the nation our junior year at Gee Dub.

I liked being at Gee Dub. I found I liked learning what others thought... up until that point I believed I was the only one with good ideas and the only one with good sense. Being smart, I always thought my ideas were always the best ideas until I arrived at Gee Dub. Every year, every day I learned something new. My days at Gee Dub were filled with learning. Yet, it was my junior year which made me aware of all the possibilities before me if only I could reach out and grab them.

Chapter 19.

June and Mo

Before we went to Spring break, I turned in my second English paper and watched as my teacher smiled at my five-page paper on the influence of the prison system on Black writers in the United States. My English teacher smiled and nodded. Five pages to address an ongoing oppressive situation which created some of the most profound and sadly unheard voice in black literature.

That same week Chauncey and I turned in our New Bill of Rights proposal to Mister Lancaster. Lancaster told everyone their projects would be hung in the halls of Gee Dub and students were going to judge them as they did with Gee Dub stickers. The more stickers the higher the grade.

"It's a popularity contest, but most things in this nation are," Mister Lancaster stated. "I will grade them all and you and you alone will be able to see my grade I gave your project. At the end of April, I will tabulate the stickers and assign a second, public grade."

The Science Fair was the last two weeks of April, after Spring break. Missus Oliver graded the projects before Spring break and the best projects were displayed at the Science Fair after Spring break.

Cash and I crafted a surprisingly intricate display of nanotubes. We learned nanotubes were the future of technology. People thought our project was interesting. Missus Oliver gave us the highest grade and Cash was smug in the outcome.

"Told you," Cash beamed as we stood at our display and watched as people streamed by to try and understand what we had done.

"I know you did," I admitted. "There's no need to gloat."

"Not gloating, just acknowledging my keen sense of observation saved us from wracking our brains over a project that is just a project of understanding."

I listened. I wanted to argue with Cash. I wanted to point out gaining knowledge was the real reward. Gaining something no one could take away from you was more important than the grade alone. I wanted to argue with Cash but seeing him standing there in his monogrammed shirt, tailored clothes and slight smirk on his face for outsmarting the system I found it hard to muster up the energy for the argument.

My last English paper of my junior year was on Education versus Indoctrination, thanks to Cash and Chauncey. I wrote about what I perceived as education and equated to the narrator in the Invisible Man. I thought, wrongly, naively, education could free me from the shackles of society had put on me from my birth. I learned the shackles were not merely restraints but reminders of the rote teachings and chasing after grades and grades alone. Rote teaching and the pursuit of grades alone was the new slavery I wrote. I had become a slave of the thing I wanted, and education had morphed into indoctrination. I did not think anymore. I just chased after a grade and only a grade. In the chasing I felt the cold metal encasings which developed on my feet and progressed toward my mind.

Yet, I concluded, in my last paper for English, the indoctrination did not stick. It did not hold. I was not made into a metallic man. I was not an automaton. I would not be a mechanical man driven by the desire for money and money alone. Instead, like the narrator in Ellison's seminal writing, I plotted my revolution and prepared for war.

When May ended most at Gee Dub prepared to head to their summer retreats. But for me and the Rescuers our summer plans had been set for months. While the majority of Gee Dub planned for vacations, summer camps and the like we, the Rescuers, had grand plans to come to fruition. That summer, my summer before I became a senior at Gee Dub, was one of the most memorable and the most significant in my high school life.

Before I explain how things made me and a dozen others become high school and national celebrities, let me tell you how my Junior year ended. After all my projects were turned in, I did not obsess over grades. Perhaps, for the first time, I was pleased with the work I had done, personally. It is a weird idea to wrap my head around, but in all the years I had been trying to be a good student I had jumped through hoops and done assignments not for me but for the grade.

My junior year I seemed to have a mental break through. I had done my best work and the grade I was given did not matter as much as before. When I checked my grades, I was pleasantly surprised to receive a high grade in US Government from Mister Lancaster and from the students who graded Chauncey and my project. I sought out Chauncey and personally thanked him for working with me. I thanked all my teachers for their hard work and prepared to become college gold.

The twelve of us, the Rescuers, had done all the groundwork. We were as prepared as we could be for the mission to succeed. All we had to do was wait for a few things to be settled.

The biggest issue was where we were going to land. If we landed in Maine, we were still in the United States and only had to deal with US laws that we might break in the release of Mo. Now, our plan did not suggest we would break any laws. What laws were there which prohibited a bunch of do-gooder kids doing good?

Now, on the other hand, if we landed in Nova Scotia, which was the preferred landing point, because there were tons of gannets there, we were suddenly in Canada. Lew and Derricka had done some research and found little to no information on any Canadian laws focused on the release of Mo on Canadian soil. But the sticking point with landing in Nova Scotia was the fact we were all minors transporting a live animal across international borders. There had to be a law about that particular subject somewhere in the Canadian legal system, but Lew and Paris had not found it. We moved ahead and hoped there was no law in releasing a gannet in Maine or Nova Scotia.

Simultaneously, we were preparing for the second week of June. One week after we had gotten out of Gee Dub and before any of the Rescuers could come up with an excuse to fly away with family anywhere, we hoped to be winging back to California victorious. The daredevils were essential, and Jayden and Kayden Smith were acrobatic masters. Allen Lattimore was physically like no one I had ever seen. He could walk on his hands from one end of the basketball court to the other. He climbed the side of a building once while waiting for a meeting on the weekend. Allen was incredible.

Based on Faith and Tanza's calculations we were aiming for a Friday or Saturday rescue. Faith had documented Mo's movements and we just wanted to be assured it would be on the cliffside Friday or Saturday.

Again, based on our calculations, if we were able to rescue Mo on Friday or Saturday, we should be able to be back no later than Saturday or Sunday.

Now, the week leading to the rescue everyone was tense. I thought it was a good thing. BB told me his basketball teams always played better when they were a little nervous. Based on that observation, we were going to crush this and be legends all at the same time.

The Monday of the planned rescue Faith, Tanza and I were in constant contact. Rome had packed the Navigator Monday.

"Auggie, have you checked in with everyone?" Faith asked.

"I have."

"Anyone questionable?" Tanza asked.

"Nope," I said.

"What about the equipment?" Tanza asked, and slightly badgering.

"We have everything."

"Okay, need you call your besties, Auggie," Tanza said. "I need you to call your besties. I got my three." Tanza paused. "Have Rome call the daredevils."

"Tell, everyone to be on call, starting tonight," Faith said.

Tuesday evening Lew, Derricka and Allen double checked the Navigator. Everything was in place. Tuesday Lew also made the various lawyers on retainer aware of our departure.

Also, there was a weather check for Friday.

Wednesday, we checked in again. Cash had acquired a car for the daredevils. The daredevils were not making the cross-continental flight. Charlie, the veterinarian, had taken the weekend off. Cash was going to pick up Tanza, the daredevils and the veterinarian and meet at Devil's Slide. The plan was for the Navigator to stay at the airport until we returned from Maine or Nova Scotia.

Thursday everyone was jumpy. Faith called. Tanza called. Cash called. Lew called. Dre called and checked in. Rome called and said be ready Friday night.

In 24 hours, we were going to make our dreams a reality.

Friday morning came and the first thing I saw on my phone was a text from Faith about the time of sunset. According to the plan we were going to give Mo two hours after sunset to find its nest and for us to be on the road to Devil's Slide.

Rome picked me up last, as I was the closest to the freeway. In the Navigator, when I climbed in were Lew, Dre, Faith, Paris, Maya, Derricka and Cue.

"Where are Cash and Tanza?"

"They are on the way. They're going to meet us at Devil's Slide," Faith smiled. "Remember?"

I was fidgety. Things were moving incredibly fast. I felt as if I was moving in slow motion and everyone around me was moving in fast motion.

I sat in the Navigator and let all the excitement and energy wash over me. I tried to be calm, but I was anything but. There was so much to take in and catalog.

We crossed the Bay Bridge and entered San Francisco. We crossed the city to reach the oceanfront. We drove down the oceanside and found San Mateo. We exited the freeway and found Devil's Slide.

In the parking lot sat a Denali. Rome parked the Navigator next to it. Cash and Tanza climbed out of the Denali. Jayden, Kayden and Allen piled out as well. The last person out of the Denali was a new face I had never seen. She was a small shouldered woman with a medium sized Afro. She had a long face that was punctuated by a broad nose and full lips.

"That's our veterinarian," Maya said.

I nodded. I noted the veterinarian had an utility belt around her waist which seemed to bristle with tools.

The veterinarian walked toward Maya and the two hugged.

"Everyone this is Charlie," Maya said. "She's our veterinarian."

Cash and Tanza turned and looked toward the daredevils. Cash walked back to the rear of the Denali. The daredevils crossed the distance and went to the rear of the Navi and grabbed their equipment.

We hiked up to the cliffside and I paused as the daredevils secured the ropes on a secure anchor. Cue filmed everything. Faith and Tanza supervised. Derricka took tons of pictures. Lew and Rome carried the extra equipment. Dre and Allen chummed up as Allen and the twins put on their helmets, goggles and padding. Each daredevil took a dozen rubber bands to band the lost bird and control it. Maya, the zoo intern and Charlie, the veterinarian were very focused and serious.

"Remember, once we capture the bird you are one hundred percent responsible for the health and well-being of that bird until we release it in Maine."

"Sounds good," Charlie said.

With everyone ready, Faith and Tanza took charge.

"Okay, Jayden, Kayden and Allen, you're up," Faith said in the dark of Devil's Slide.

We had gathered on the cliffside with all the equipment. Lew and Derricka oversaw the daredevil equipment.

Rome gave two PVC tubes to each daredevil. All three were expected to wrangle Mo. The leader was Kayden. He was the first to go over the lip of the cliff like he was going for a walk in the park. I stood back and allowed those of braver stuff to do the dirty work.

I stood on the cliffside in the darkness for nearly fifteen minutes before I heard the daredevils hooting and hollering and a few minutes later Allen popped over the top. Jayden was second and he had Mo. Kayden was third and clapping his brother on his shoulder.

Charlie, the vet, was handed Mo in the PVC tube. In the dark I could see its pointy beak sticking out of the top of the open tube. The bird's feet were barely visible.

Cue was in the way of everyone. He filmed everything. He had nearly fallen off the cliff twice trying to document the capture of Mo. Thankfully, Dre was close and caught him.

Lew was giddy. Faith was jumping up and down. Cash, all at once, was serious. Tanza, the Rockstar, who had been there and done that, had hugged me for a long moment. I hugged her back and breathed in her candy sweet perfume off her neck and snake braids.

The quest, which had begun two years before, was now in a five-foot PVC pipe with its deadly beak sticking out. Paris and Lew sat on the ground exhausted. The Smith brothers were breaking down their rappelling equipment and high fiving each other like they had won the Superbowl. I wanted to cry.

Suddenly Faith was hugging me. I hugged her back. It was a natural reaction.

I released Faith and looked at the magically attractive girl who had squeezed me like a pack of Charmin. She had those apple cheeks, the straight nose, the dark arched eyebrows over her mischievous eyes and those full, full lips which in a flash seemed kissable.

She smiled. I smiled as well. I looked at Faith for a long moment. I felt something with Faith in that moment, I didn't know what or how to describe it, but I knew Paris noticed.

There was movement all around me but for that long moment I just looked into the big brown eyes of Faith. I know how it sounds. I was not supposed to be crushing on Faith.

"We got to get moving," Tanza said. "We got to get to the airport."

Paris and Lew and Derricka started grabbing the equipment. Allen, Jayden and Kayden were shedding their helmets, goggles, and padding.

"Cash, make the call," Faith said smiling awkwardly and looking away.

"I thought we had blown it," one of the twins said. "We landed just out of reach of the big ugly."

"Thankfully, Jayden was there. He snuck up on the big ugly and squeezed its wings against its body while Allen banded the beak." He paused, as Charlie and Maya walked the PVC encased gannet toward the Navigator. "That was it. I slipped the PVC over the big galoot and it did not struggle or fight after that."

"Easy pickings," Kayden laughed.

Paris stepped between me and Faith. Paris looked over Faith's shoulder and rolled her eyes at me. I looked for Dre or Rome for a moment. I paused, I felt Faith and I had something...a connection?

"Got it," Cash said, turning on his heels and nearly bumping into Tanza. He pulled his cell phone from his pocket. Tanza too spun on her heels and promptly everyone was in motion. The only ones not in motion were the daredevils.

Rome clapped his hands in the faces of the daredevils to bring them back to earth. Everyone packed out and from the cliffside back to the vehicles.

All the equipment we had brought we packed out and back to the Denali and Navigator. Rome and Derricka climbed into the Navigator. I climbed into the third-row seat behind Lew, Cue, Paris and Faith.

The trunk was filled straight away with all the equipment we could store.

"We rolling."

"Are the others coming," Paris asked.

"Cash, how big is the plane you got?"

"It can fit twenty comfortably," Cash smirked.

"They can if they want. Not everyone signed on for the flight."

"Who didn't?"

"Well, the Smith brothers and Allen only wanted to catch a bird. They liked the adventure and danger."

"What about Dre? Or Paris?"

"Don't talk about me, Auggie," Paris said with a growl. "You know I'm down for a plane ride."

Rome was under the wheel. Lew seated behind him. The pair were giddy and laughing like little girls. Somehow Derricka and Dre were sitting in the same passenger seat. Lew, Paris and Faith were seated in the second row of the Lincoln. Cue was there too. He was filming everything and everyone. I sat in the rear of the SUV with Charlie and Maya and the gannet in the PVC tube. Charlie was monitoring the captured bird.

"We have about eight hours until things get dicey," Charlie announced. She had her phone out and on countdown toward zero.

Rome, the driver, nodded and picked up speed. Paris gave Rome the stink eye.

"Don't kill us getting there okay?"

"I have improved my driving skills," Rome snarled.

We were on the freeway and headed to the airport. Rome drove expertly. He switched lanes as we got close to the airport. I held onto the passenger seat as Rome drove a little faster.

"Can you believe we did it?"

I shook my head.

"So, what happens when we get to the coast?"

"Hell, man, that's the easy part," Maya said. "We just release the bird, and it flies around and eats and gets stronger before his family arrives, and he reunites." Maya paused. "Happy ending."

The Lincoln Navigator circled the airport and found the entrance to the private airport. Dre leaned forward and pointed toward the hangar just to the right of the main air tower in the private airport just to the left of the international terminal.

The Denali was parking next to the hangar.

"Pull in there," Derricka said.

The Navigator parked on the side of the hangar next to the Denali. Cash was the first out of the Denali. The daredevils climbed out of the Denali horsed around as everyone in the Navigator climbed out of the SUV.

Cash walked to the office and I followed for some reason. He was greeted by a black man with a neatly cut fade. He was dressed in sneakers, jeans and a cartoon T-shirt. He looked nothing like a pilot.

"My man, Cash," the stranger said as everyone gathered behind Cash.

"Are you ready?"

"Always ready," the stranger said and smiled. "We can be wheels up in ten," the stranger said, heading toward his office inside the hangar.

Cash looked back and beckoned us to follow. He walked toward the sleek white and blue trimmed private jet with a solid blue tail. The steps were down and welcoming.

A few of the Rescuers climbed on the plane.

The pilot, the man Cash had spoken to came out with another man.

"This is Parker," Cash said to the daredevils and anyone who was listening. "He will drive the Denali back to Oakland. He will drop you wherever you want." Cash paused. "Grab your stuff and you're in Parker's hands."

In ten minutes, the airplane was taking to the air. Everyone was a little surprised at the plushness of the plane.

"We should be landing no later than six o'clock in the morning," Tanza said. "Cash said the pilot will try and get clearance to land in Nova Scotia. If that is a no go then we have to land in Maine."

"Of course, we want to land in Nova Scotia," Faith said. "But if we have to land in Maine we will just drive to the coast and release Mo and hope. He will be on the right coast and there will be more of his kind flying around."

The plane headed east and before we crossed Nevada most of the Rescuers were sleeping. I tried to stay awake. I checked in on Mo and Charlie.

"How we doing?"

Charlie, the olive-skinned woman with a curly Afro framing her angular face looked up. She had thick eyebrows and small eyes which sat above her broad nose and full lips.

"He seems stable," the veterinarian said. She looked up from the PVC tube and at me. "When do you think we will land?"

I looked back and offered the last time Tanza had said.

"What happens when we release Mo?"

"Mo?"

"That's what we call him," I laughed.

She nodded. "Well, it's pretty simple. We release it in the direction of the ocean and after a little bit it will look for its kind. That's it."

"That's it?"

"Yeah, that's it," Charlie said.

"Well, keep me informed if there are any changes."

I looked back and saw Faith sleeping in her chair. Paris was by her, sleeping as well. The only person it seemed other than me and Charlie still energetic and focused was Cue. He was filming people sleeping in the interior of the airplane.

I looked back at Charlie.

I climbed to my feet and walked toward my seat feeling a wave of fatigue flow through me. I held back a yawn. I noted Cash and Tanza were awake.

"Better get some sleep," Cash said. "We're not even two hours into the flight. We are trying to lock down the landing."

"Yeah, I know," I said. "When do you think you'll know?"

"Hopefully, soon," Cash smiled.

Tanza sat down and stretched, preparing to go to sleep.

"If anything changes Marlon, will tell us," Cash said.

With that, I walked to my seat across from Faith. Lew was snoring audibly. Dre and Rome were asleep in their seats. Paris turned to get comfortable. Derricka was sprawled out and sleeping like she was at home. Cue walked up and down the aisle filming everyone.

"Might want to get some rest," I said to Cue. I rubbed at my eyes and yawned.

I sat down and before I could say, "Boo," my eyes were closing. In seconds I was sleeping soundly. I suppose it had a lot to do with the buildup to the moment of standing on the cliff and hoping for the best, but I slept. The sleep was a good deep sleep. I slept and heard sounds, pictured images that never sharpened into anything I could recognize and just floated in the darkness of slumber.

Hours passed. I slept. The Rescuers rested.

The next thing I recall is Dre shaking me awake. I opened my eyes and had to take a minute to recall I was not home, but on a plane headed east. On the plane were my friends and a bird and a veterinarian and a pilot named Marlon. I blinked and rubbed at my eyes.

"We're close," someone said.

"We-we-we're close," Dre repeated. Lew beside him. Rome loomed in from behind Dre.

"Wake up sleepy head, we got some work to do," Rome said with a big smile.

I rubbed at my eyes and stretched my body to its full length.

"What time is it?"

"Don't know," Lew laughed. "I sort of lost track with all the time zones. In Cali I think it is three or four o'clock in the morning. Here," Lew waved to the interior of the plane. "I'm not sure."

"We've been on one hell of an adventure," Cash said to Cue, who was up and filming again.

"All right, you lot, buckle up, we are about to land," Marlon, the pilot announced from the cockpit.

"Land," I repeated. I looked to Faith who was all smiles. Tanza and Paris were seated near me. "Where are we landing?"

"I think we've been cleared to land in Nova Scotia," Faith said, leaning close to me and smiling. I nodded in reply. Nova Scotia? We were going to Canada. Did we need passports? Didn't matter. We didn't have passports. Well, I knew I didn't have a passport. I knew Lew, Dre and Rome didn't have passports either.

I turned to Cash. "Cash, we have a car waiting?"

"Yeah, man, don't worry," Cash smiled. Tanza and Cash were seated and lounging in their chairs, just a few feet from me.

"Cue, sit down and buckle up," said Derricka.

I looked back and Cue reluctantly sat down and buckled up for the landing.

In a few minutes we were on the ground and headed for a hangar.

"Ever been out of the states," asked Tanza.

I shook my head, no.

"Most of us haven't," Faith replied. "Most of us haven't been on a plane before."

Chapter 20.

We landed in Yarmouth, Nova Scotia. The airport was small more like a private airport than an international airport. The coast was visible from the airport. Marlon guided the plane down the landing strip and turned it toward the bigger hangar and powered down the engines. The pilot climbed out of his seat and opened the cabin door.

Cash and Tanza were the first to climb to their feet.

"I'll gas up the plane and do a check and text you our flight plan," Marlon, the pilot said, just loud enough to be heard.

We deplaned. Cash walked to a waiting dark blue Escalade parked outside the hangar. Cash climbed in and grabbed the car keys. He also unlocked the back of the Escalade. The Escalade was bigger than the Navigator. It was wider and there seemed to be more interior room.

From the airport, we could have walked to the coast, but the plan was to find Mo birds which looked like him.

Rome insisted on driving. Now, Cash had arranged for us to have an Escalade and the two bickered over who deserved to drive to the coast. Thankfully, Tanza, the final word, spoke up after the kerfuffle began and Faith or Paris brought the problem to her attention.

"You idiots, there's an easy solution," Tanza said. "Flip a coin. Whoever wins drives us to the coast. When we drive back the other one drives us back."

That settled that.

Charlie and Maya loaded Mo in the back of the Escalade and sat watching his progress. Everyone climbed in after them. Cue was the last into the SUV.

"All right, we're off," smiled Rome. He put the Escalade in gear, and we headed toward the coast.

The ride away from the airport and to the closest water source was on a two-lane highway which gave way to the lakes and coast from the airport in Nova Scotia. The drive took nearly forty-five minutes, one way as we tried to find the perfect spot to release Mo.

"Why don't we release him here," asked Paris, a little bored and annoyed.

"You know the reason," Faith said, with a shake of her head.

We found a one lane road which took us to a sign which read: Plymouth. The ride was not calm or quiet there seemed to be a dozen loud and heated arguments as to where to release Mo.

"Look," Derricka said, pointing toward the left. Everyone seeing Derricka pointing looked left. There, to the left of Rome were the gray headed and black headed birds. There were easily a dozen of the birds gathered near the cliff edge.

"I think we can stop the car," Lew said to Rome. Rome nodded. He pulled onto a quiet road which seemed to go on forever and was bordered by a rickety fence.

We all climbed out of the Escalade and Charlie and Maya took Mo in the PVC tube out of the Escalade. Cue followed and filmed everything.

Charlie and Maya carried Mo in the PVC tube to the field on the other side of the rickety fence. Lew, Mister Hug-A-Tree, insisted on being there for the release. Everyone pulled their cellphones out and recorded everything from that moment.

Rome and Dre just smiled like jack-o-lanterns. I watched from a safe distance. Having seen Mo's beak and recalling what Mister Pope had said about its ability to poke out an eye, it seemed the smartest plan. Faith and Paris stood nearby. Cash and Tanza leaned on the Escalade.

In the field Charlie and Maya gently placed the tube on the grass. Lew was just there, a third wheel. I chuckled at Lew's awkwardness. Cue was close to the action, but like us, standing at a safe distance from the bird in the PVC cylinder.

"Here goes," Maya yelled. Lew looked back and gave us the thumbs up. I couldn't help but shake my head at Lew being with the veterinarian and her intern. Lew just loved nature and would not missing the moment of Mo's release. Quincy was circling like an investigative reporter looking for crucial missing details.

We all watched as Charlie and Maya pushed Mo out of the top of the white PVC cylinder and his beak then head emerged. Maya removed the rubber bands the daredevils had put on in San Francisco. As soon as its head could turn left or right it squawked. Lew jumped back with the first sound of Mo since California. Charlie, ever the professional, pushed Mo's feet from the bottom of the cylinder and all of a sudden Mo's wings were freed and it was flapping on the ground to escape the tube.

Maya and Charlie retreated as Mo finally freed himself. Lew seeing Charlie and Maya backing up retreated as well. Quincy tried to get a good picture, but he started to back up as well.

The release of the bird was a little disappointing. I had thought Charlie and Maya and the bird might hug or kiss or something. The bird got to its feet and wobbled around a bit and seemed to gain its balance. It then stared at Charlie and Maya and Cue who was circling all of them. Mo looked at Lew and then us all for half a minute. It opened its bird beak and closed it.

It just looked at us with those big bird eyes and though I knew it did not know we had saved it from a life all alone without any other bird like it on the west coast I wanted it to say something, do something for all our hard work. But it just turned and looked at Charlie and Maya, then us, then the ocean and the sun and went flying off. It was a bit anti-climatic for a goodbye.

"That's it," Dre said.

"That's it," Cash said.

There was a long pause as everyone tried to take in the accomplishment of returning Mo to the Atlantic. Tanza and Cash leaned on the Escalade and looked out at the horizon.

"I'm hungry," Rome said breaking the silence.

I looked at Charlie and Maya as Lew and Cue trekked back to the Escalade. Lew handed me the PVC tube where Mo had been encased. I smiled and walked back to the Escalade. Cue was filming me with the tube.

"Think we can stop filming Cue," I said.

"Not yet," Cue said. He ran ahead and spoke with Tanza and Faith.

"All right, everyone we got one more photo and Cue says that's it. He wants us to take a picture in front of the Escalade. Then we get some food and head back home."

"Easy peasy," Dre said.

"Easy peasy," I said, with a smile.

We all walked back to the Escalade and Cue filmed us coming around the black SUV like superstars. Tanza was directing. It took us all of five minutes to climb in the Escalade just so. Thankfully, we were too tired to argue. It was still just four o'clock in the morning in California.

Cash drove us back to the airport with a detour and stop at A&W Canada. It was the only thing open at that hour.

When we returned to the airport there was a note on the plane.

Cash read the note and twisted his lips as if what he read left a bad taste in his mouth.

"What's going on?"

"It's nothing serious," Cash explained. "Marlon needs a few hours to recover before flying us back to Cali."

"A few hours," squeaked Paris.

"How long is that?"

"He says he'll be ready to go at two o'clock, eastern standard time."

"That's six hours," Derricka squealed.

"What are we going to do in Nova Scotia for six hours?"

Faith and Tanza laughed.

We had just eaten. We were bored. We had six hours to kill. And we were suddenly in Nova Scotia on a layover.

Faith and Tanza Googled what to do in Yarmouth, Nova Scotia and found 15 things to do.

We looked at the list and with Faith and Tanza in charge we knew they wanted to see all 15 things.

"Before you guys start thinking that we're going to be doing some tour of Nova Scotia, I am not doing it. You can leave me here. I'll just sack out in the plane until we take off," Rome said. He shook his head and headed for the hangar and the plane. He stopped and turned around. "If you get some food bring me back something to tide me over until we get back to California."

Rome voted with his feet. Everyone gathered at the hangar had to suddenly make decisions. Faith and Tanza had to convince the remaining Rescuers to go on a tour with them. They needed a driver. The most important person suddenly was Cash.

"I don't know if I want to see what Yarmouth has to offer," Derricka admitted.

"I'm with you," Maya said with a smile. "I just want to rest and get back home."

Dre nodded his head in agreement.

"There can't be that much to do here," Derricka said. "I mean, we could walk to the coast pretty easily."

"Don't know if I want to just sit in a hangar and look at the coast for six hours," said Paris. "Let's go do something."

"What are the choices?"

"We can go to the lighthouse. There's a park," Tanza began, with a shake of her head. "There's a Firefighters Museum; a brewery, where we could get something to eat; there's something called the W. Laurence Sweeney Fishery Museum and if you go to Yarmouth you have to go to the Murray Manor Art and Cultural House."

"I don't want to go to a lighthouse," Derricka said.

"Pass," said Dre.

"We ain't in school. I don't want to go on a field trip," Cash said.

I shook my head.

"Well, going to the city center gives us a better choice of food," Faith pivoted. "We can get something to eat that's not coming out of a vending machine."

Cash's ears perked up with Faith's pivot.

"Well, if we can get some lunch then that might be worth the trip."

"Okay, the way I see it some of us want to go and see what is here," Derricka said. "Not me. Count me out."

The first fifteen minutes of the first two hours in Nova Scotia there had to be an argument.

"Okay, who's going with us?"

"Auggie, you coming?"

Reluctantly, I went with Cash, Tanza, Faith, Cue and Paris. Lew was a welcome sight to see climbing to his feet and trotting to the Escalade in the final minute before we drove toward the bustling city of Yarmouth.

Cash wheeled the Escalade through the quiet pastural lands of Yarmouth like a champ. We drove leisurely toward the city northeast of the airport. Once in the city limits, we parked in what was downtown Yarmouth. The only way we determined it to be downtown was the storefronts which appeared on the horizon and almost immediately reminded me of those old western towns in movies with a hardware store, a jail, a bank and a bar. If a horse drawn wagon or cowboy would have stepped out of one of the stores I would not have been surprised.

For those of us who had never flown or been out of the country Yarmouth was a little disappointing is an understatement. The biggest hotel in the port town was Comfort Inn. The biggest fast-food establishment in the town was McDonald's. Cash parked the Escalade in front of hardware store which seemed to have defied time and convention and was still stuck in the 1960's. We climbed out of the Escalade and were instantly aware of the difference of being in Yarborough. There were no black people on the street when we arrived in the sleepy little town.

We walked around the small town and though it could be early found the sleepy town busy, if twenty or thirty people walking the streets of Yarmouth was deemed busy. We watched the locals try to figure out how we had appeared in their town. We were an attraction suddenly for the people of Yarmouth.

Tanza and Faith tried to put lipstick on the pig of disappointment of the port town which was Yarmouth on a Saturday morning.

"We can go to Frost Park since we are here and see what fun stuff there is there," Tanza said.

"Tanza, you see what we seeing, right?"

"I think we might want to get some food and get the hell out of here," Cue said as he filmed the locals looking at us.

"I think you might be misjudging Yarmouth," Tanza attempted.

"You seen Get Out," I said. "This is one of those type of places. We need to get the hint and fall back."

"I'm with Auggie," Lew said. "This place kind of gives me the creeps."

"Well, let's go to Wendy's and get some food, since we're here."

"Okay," Faith asked.

We reluctantly gave in and walked down the street to Wendy's. We texted and asked Rome and the others what they wanted. We told them via text we were at Wendy's.

We got our order and headed back to the Escalade. My heart nearly fell out of my chest when I saw the Yarmouth Police Department police car parked by the Escalade.

A white man who looked like Andy Griffin was standing by the SUV as we walked up. He smiled and nodded at us.

"Hey there," the man said, with a smile and another nod.

"What can we do for you officer?"

"Well, as you probably have noticed, Yarmouth isn't that big," the white man said with that smile on his face. As he spoke, I could see him looking us over.

"Was wondering what brings you to Yarmouth?"

"The Escalade," said Paris, indignant.

"We are just visiting for a few hours before we head back to California," Tanza said, elbowing Paris in the chest.

"California," the police officer said with a nod of his head.

"Yep," said Cash who stepped forward. "Is there a problem officer?"

"No problem, son," the officer said. "How old are you?"

"Me? I'm seventeen," Cash said.

"Who's driving the vehicle?"

"Why," I asked.

Cue opened his cell phone and tapped the camera app.

The smile faded with my question. The friendly and curious man disappeared. He was replaced by a steely eyed policeman standing in front of us.

"We are heading back to the airport, to wait for our plane to be fueled up, officer," Tanza smiled.

The policeman smiled and nodded. He gestured to the Escalade and Cash unlocked the Escalade and we all climbed in. I was one of the last to climb into the SUV. The police officer walked to his squad car and reached into his open car window. I watched as he pulled out a microphone to his car radio as Cash backed the Escalade out of the parking space.

I turned and looked at everyone in the SUV, suddenly tense. Lew just shook his head. Paris was at the window looking to see what the policeman was doing as the Escalade headed toward the airport. Cue was filming inside of the SUV. Faith was beside me and quiet. Tanza and Cash, the usual calm and cool pair even seemed tense.

Once on the two-lane road back to the airport the Escalade passengers all seemed to take a collective breath.

"That was crazy," Faith finally said. I nodded. The interior of the Escalade went from library quiet to raucous. I leaned across Faith and tapped Paris.

"You guys might want to contact those lawyers," I said. "Opie was calling someone when we pulled away. Figure we will have company soon."

"What," Cue said.

"Auggie saw the po-po calling for backup."

"What happened," Tanza said looking back into the passenger seat. I sat back and watched as everyone talked about what I had tried to tell Paris and only Paris.

"You think they coming for us," Faith said, her voice shook just a little.

"Don't know," I admitted.

When we arrived back at the airport, we knocked ninety minutes off the six hours of waiting.

Lew and Paris conferred. I sat and ate my food with Faith and Dre.

For the next twenty minutes in Nova Scotia we explained to Rome, Derricka, Dre and Maya what it must have felt like to live in the 1960's in America.

"So, who paid for the food?"

Tanza explained why she had bought our food with a credit card. Tanza tried to explain to everyone in Canada did not use US dollars often, only in the bigger cities.

For the next thirty minutes in Nova Scotia Tanza had to explain to Rome, Lew, Dre, Paris and anyone who would listen why she paid for the food. The idea of US dollars not being accepted was alien to so many. I understood the concept of being in Canada, but we were still speaking English and that small detail was the square peg in the round hole that did not fit.

"But why did your credit card work?"

"I don't know," Tanza said, frustrated. "I think the banks have some kind of arrangement. All I know is that credit works everywhere."

"Is that why adults want credit cards so much?"

Tanza shrugged.

The last two hours before Marlon returned to the plane were less than quiet as people napped, slept and walked around the airplane hangar. Lew found a basketball and Cash, Rome and Dre played a pick-up game behind the hangar on one of those movable basketball rims which had a weighted foot and wheels to move it around.

No one was LeBron or Magic Johnson, but they talked like they were anytime they didn't have the ball. They played 21 and the game got boring really quickly when the fourth airball from the fourth different player hit the ground without hitting the rim. I tried to look at it as entertaining. The trash talk was definitely entertaining. It came down as a way to wile away the time. I watched for about thirty minutes before I got bored. After Lew hit a jumper and the score was 2-0, I climbed to my feet and walked around the hangar.

We were nearly a couple of hours back from Yarmouth when I found Faith and Tanza sitting on some pallets in the shade of the hangar looking at the screens of their phones. I smiled. They had found an outlet to charge their phones.

"Oh, oh," I said, seeing four Yarmouth police cars drive into the airport and come across the airfield.

"Where's Lew," I said pointing to the police cars. "Or Paris?"

"Oh, snap," said Tanza.

Faith jumped up from the pallet and snatched her phone cord out of the hidden outlet. She scrambled. "Paris," Faith screamed. In a moment, Faith was running to the corner of the hangar.

The four police cars stopped in front of the plane hangar. The policemen climbed out of the cars and looked around the hangar. No one had drawn guns, but their hands were on the butts of their service weapons.

"Relax, kids," one of the police officers announced, lifting his empty hands.

Tanza, Cash, Cue, Rome, Derricka, Dre, Charlie and Maya and I were gathered quickly at the front of the hangar. I was separated from Rome and Dre and for a moment I thought to just walk to the side of my friends. I also thought I wanted to be near Cue. He was filming everything. The eight police who gathered us watched us as the smiling white policeman we had met in Yarmouth earlier was among the eight.

"So, what are you doing in Yarmouth," said one of the policemen talking beside me to Maya.

When the policemen assigned to talk to me asked me questions, I chose not to answer. No one was willing to answer. Of the nine of us we all played dumb. We didn't have to do that too long.

Lew and Paris walked into the plane's hangar with two lawyers dressed in suits and ties. One of the lawyers was carrying a briefcase and sported a luxury high priced watch I had only seen in rap videos. He was a diamond faced man with strangely and perfectly combed dark brown hair. The diamond faced man was wearing a blue suit and a powder blue collared shirt without a tie and black leather lace up shoes. In his ear was a big diamond earring.

The other lawyer was a little older and taller than the man beside him and looked a bit like a game show host with a big forehead, beady eyes, a slightly hooked nose and thin lips. He was wearing a gray suit, white collared shirt, gray silk tie and brown leather shoes. He wore horn rimmed glasses and had a five o'clock shadow of salt and pepper beard.

Lew and Paris were smiling from ear-to-ear on the side of the taller lawyer. Paris looked smug and confident. Lew nodded as he walked to us.

"Gentlemen, may I help you," the older lawyer said. "We are attorneys at law, retained by our clients while in Nova Scotia. I need to point out constables, they are all under eighteen years of age and thus should not be interrogated without proper supervision or legal representation."

The police were cowed by the appearance of our lawyers. The police spoke to our lawyers and we listened. After about an hour the younger attorney looked at Lew and Paris and gave them the thumbs up.

Cue filmed the entire incident. He was live streaming the incident on several social networks. Derricka and Tanza had their phones out and recording the incident as well.

Fifteen minutes after the lawyers had shown up the police had gone. Ten minutes after that the lawyers had gone. It was just us again waiting for Marlon and the plane.

With a half hour until the flight Marlon, the pilot, drove up in a convertible Jaguar driven by a muscular bald guy the color of peanut butter, wearing sunglasses on his flat face. The driver was dressed in a short-sleeved shirt which showed off his incredibly gigantic biceps. Next to the bodybuilder sat Marlon, wearing sunglasses and smiling. In the rear of the convertible was a small faced sand colored woman with curly black hair who was wearing a blue blouse.

The convertible pulled up to the hangar and Marlon climbed out. He helped the shapely small faced woman from the rear of the car and sat her in the passenger seat. Marlon reached across the woman and exchanged a fist bump with the bodybuilding driver.

"Everybody ready," Marlon asked as he walked into the hangar. He did not wait for an answer from anyone. Marlon walked to the small office in the private hangar. Before he entered the office, Marlon turned to and said, "Where's Cash?"

Cash gathered everyone and we loaded the plane.

The plane ride back to the west coast was uneventful.

The plane flew smoothly and as it did all those who had been raring to go started to doze. I could not help but smile.

Faith saw me smiling.

"What are you doing," Faith asked.

"I am trying to figure out who's going to sleep next," I said. "It is kind of something to do."

Faith and I bet on who would be the next to fall asleep between Rome and Lew.

"I have to go with Lew," I said. "That guy loves to sleep."

"I'm betting on Rome."

Lew was the first to fall asleep and start snoring. Rome was the second. Dre was next and laying back in his chair like he was at the beach. Derricka was lying across two seats and over Cue. Cue had his head against the wall of the plane. Charlie and Maya were asleep as well.

I climbed out of my seat and went to the bathroom. When I returned Paris and Faith were smiling and watching me.

"What's up?"

"We're not even halfway there," Paris said, with a shake of her head. "Faith told me about your sleep game. Who is going to go to sleep first between us?"

I shook my head.

"I think it's probably going to be you," Paris said with a sneer.

She was leaning on the back of the passenger seat looking at a sleeping Dre who was trying to get comfortable.

Paris turned around and smiled at me. We were jetting westward. Faith and Paris smiled and looked at me like they had a secret. I didn't want to give into their game. So, I changed the unsaid topic.

"If you could go anywhere, where would you go?" I was looking at Paris to see how she thought. I also wanted to put her on the grill, a little.

"I don't know," Paris said. "Maybe down south. I got family that live in Louisiana."

"How 'bout you?""

Faith smiled and bit her lower lip, thinking. I watched her biting her lower lip and had to blink and look away. Paris looked at me oddly. Paris looked at me and pointed back at Faith, with a head shake.

"I suppose I would want to go to New York," Faith said. "I never been there."

I nodded.

"How 'bout you?"

I shrugged. I didn't really have any real destination I wanted to go to, specifically. I pinched my lips, for a moment.

"I suppose I would like to go to Africa to see a real rhinoceros in the wild. I would love to see a herd of rhinos running on the plains." I paused, seeing Paris and Faith looking at me, curiously. "You asked."

"I did ask."

Paris and Faith giggled.

I yawned. I was tired. I listened to Faith and Paris, but I found myself being pushed down by an invisible hand into a chair.

"You should get some rest. We have a long flight home."

I nodded.

Paris just shook her head. I looked at Faith and Paris and as I sat in the comfort of the passenger seat my body relaxed. My muscles, which were tense a moment before, eased into the cushions of the seat. It was as if my entire body exhaled, and I could not say anything, I heard Faith's voice ask a question as I was falling asleep.

"What are you going to do for the summer," she asked, and I was falling asleep.

I slept most of the way back. I woke and found Paris sleeping next to me. Faith was asleep as well.

"We're nearly home," Rome said.

"We're just over Utah, Cash just said," Lew said.

I nodded. I tried to calculate how far we were from landing. Maybe, we were less than two hours from landing.

When we were preparing to descend and land the plane seemed to bristle with anticipation. We had been away from the Bay Area for a full day. I know I longed to be in familiar settings having been further away than I ever imagined. I had gone to another country. I had landed in Yarmouth and eaten at an A&W Canada. There were so many memories, but I had to admit I would be looking forward to sleeping in my own bed.

The private plane landed and as I exited the plane. I thanked Marlon the pilot. It seemed important. As we made our way to

Rome's Lincoln Navigator I reached out to Cash and clapped him on his shoulder to get his attention.

"Cash, thanks," I said.

He nodded.

We drove from the airport and back to the East Bay. Rome dropped off Cash and Tanza at the international airport where their drivers were waiting. Faith and Tanza hugged. They had become fast friends. Derricka and Tanza carpooled together. As Cash exited the Navigator, I thanked Cash again. Cue asked to be dropped off near Gee Dub. Charlie and Maya were dropped off downtown. Faith and Paris got out near Lake Merritt.

When Faith and Paris climbed out of the SUV, I climbed out also. I stood by the SUV unsure. Faith smiled and stepped toward me. I reached out and Faith and I hugged.

"Thanks, Auggie," Faith said. "This has been an incredible and memorable year."

"It has," I said. "It has." I cleared my throat.

We hugged for about ten seconds longer and then I released her.

Paris smiled and shook her head. I looked in the direction Paris was looking. I saw Dre and Lew peering out of the Navi's windows. Rome was watching via the side mirror.

I smirked.

"At least, with this one, you don't have to worry about her breaking your heart," Paris said.

Faith and Paris walked toward the lake. About ten steps away Faith turned and smiled and waved goodbye. I waved back.

I climbed back in the SUV.

"What was that?"

"Are you and Faith now together,"

"When did all this happen?"

I shook my head in response. I didn't have any real answers. There was no use in trying to explain.

"Let it go," Rome said. Rome pointed the Navigator toward the freeway and after getting on and driving four exits he exited and headed toward my house.

Dre smiled silently at me from the passenger seat.

Lew reached out and nodded and placed a hand on my shoulder as if he understood.

I closed my eyes. I was tired. We were all tired. We had done something, and no one knew anything about it.

It was just an hour before the sun began to set when I finally returned home.

Rome pulled the Navigator to the curb and I just sat. No one in the crew moved.

I sat and listened to the Lincoln's engine trembling under the hood. I did not grab the door handle. I just sat there.

"Thanks, everybody," I said. "We did it. We saved Mo. We came. We saw. We conquered."

"Auggie, you were right," Lew said.

"Yeah," Dre said.

"Man, Auggie, we were on the east coast just a couple of hours ago. We were in Canada. Can you believe it?"

We celebrated in the Lincoln Navigator. We screamed and shouted and laughed and hugged. After we stopped screaming and shouting, I grabbed the door handle. Lew was the first to notice and stop his smiling. Rome and Dre quieted.

"You going?"

"Yeah, I need to make sure my mom didn't call the cops and report me kidnapped."

"Yeah, I suppose we all need to do that," Lew said.

"Yeah," I said. "Thanks again." I climbed out of the Navigator and closed the door.

The passenger side windows rolled down and Dre and Lew looked out.

"I'll call you guys later."

"Okay," Dre smiled.

Rome put the Navigator in gear and the large SUV slid into the lane and pulled away from the curb.

I smiled. I turned on my heel and walked up the three stairs to our house and across the short wooden porch to our front door. I fished out my keys and unlocked the door and entered my quiet home.

I dropped my backpack at the door and headed to the living room. I grabbed the remote control and turned on the TV. I stretched out on the couch and before long the TV was watching me sleep.

"Auggie, wake up," I heard someone say. I opened my eyes and there was my mom looking down at me.

I blinked. I rubbed at my eyes and sat up.

"You okay, sweetheart?"

"Yeah," I said.

"How was your overnight?"

"It was good," I said. My mom patted my cheek and walked into the kitchen.

"You hungry? We're having," my mom began only to pause. She was a room away. A wall separated us. I heard the refrigerator door swing open. "Chicken and green beans and corn."

I smiled and nodded in the living room.

"Yeah, that's great," I said. "That's great."

Epilogue.

Our fifteen minutes of fame? We were suddenly being interviewed everywhere. I cannot count all the interviews I did after returning from Nova Scotia about racial profiling. The videos of the police encounter outside the airport hangar was a social media buzz. When we landed in California Tanza found her fans irate. She was asked to talk about what happened on half a dozen social media networks. Tanza, Derricka and anyone who wanted to discuss the incident. I was reluctant to be interviewed. I picked my moments.

At the end of the month Tanza and Cash invited us all over to Cash's house in the hills to see the thirty-minute video Cue had made of the rescue of Mo. It was the rough cut of what Cue was working on. Cue promised to have a final version before the end of the summer.

Rome picked me up about an hour before sunset. When I climbed in the Navi Faith was sitting there all smiles with Paris and Derricka. Lew and Allen, the daredevil, were sitting in the third seat. Dre was in the passenger seat next to Rome.

Faith and I were talking every day and still just friends. I wanted to be sure not to screw things up. To make sure I decided to go slow, real slow. Faith seemed to understand.

I sat next to Allen and everyone seemed to hold their breath as I said hello to Faith and everyone in the SUV.

There were a lot of whispers and side glances and talking under the breath as we drove to Cash's house. I sat between Lew and Allen.

"Auggie, what is going on," Allen whispered to me.

"Got me," I said, playing dumb.

"They were saying that someone is crushing on someone in the Navi, but they don't think he's ready to pull the trigger and prove it."

"Prove it?"

"Yeah," Allen whispered. "A kiss is proof they said."

I nodded. I sat and thought about what Allen said. I wondered if Allen had been told to say those exact words to see what I would do. My mind reeled.

Rome drove us to Cash's house which sat on the top of the hill behind ten-foot-high ornate gates. This house was bigger, more palatial and grander than Rome's house. The driveway was circular and sported a Bentley and a Porsche Cayenne. Rome parked the Lincoln behind the Porsche SUV.

We climbed out of the Navigator and found Tanza standing outside of the house.

"Come on, everyone, we've been waiting," Tanza said, with a big smile.

Everyone followed Tanza into Cash's house and past three adults sitting at a table talking. The house was more like an auditorium, than a house. Everything was so big and shiny. Tanza led us to the private theater where all the Rescuers were waiting. We hugged and fist bumped and the like. It was good to see Cue, Charlie, Maya and the Smith brothers again.

"Everyone sit down. If you want something there is popcorn, hotdogs and soda in the concession area," Cash smiled.

Of course, Rome, Dre and Lew made a beeline for the concession stand and came back with popcorn, hotdogs and drinks. I walked to the concession stand and got a hotdog and something to drink. Faith got some popcorn and a hotdog.

"Okay, everyone sit down," Cash said.

We all sat and prepared to watch the story of our expedition to save Mo from a solitary life on the wrong ocean.

"I still have tons of film," Cue gushed. "I just made a highlight reel for everyone. It sort of hangs together. There's a story there and all. People can see what we did," the filmmaker said and sat down.

The lights went down. The small private theater got silent.

Faith leaned over and whispered, "This is so exciting."

The title of the documentary was: The Rescuers. Suddenly, all our names appeared.

Cue began the documentary with us in the first meeting on the football bleachers. He weaved the story of the mission and all the work it took to recruit and find the right people to make the mission a success. Faith, Tanza and I were mentioned as the project leaders. Through the entirety of the film there was an emphasis on the team element of the mission. "No one was non-essential. Everyone was essential," Faith said. There was a snippet of me explaining what we needed to do to rescue Mo. The daredevils were introduced. The documentary detailed all the steps and the rescue and the flight to Nova Scotia. The release of Mo was a little artsy as the gangly bird stared at us and finally flew away. The documentary ended with the Rescuers at the Escalade exhausted and happy. The credits rolled.

Everyone clapped. I stood up and spun around and just shook my head at Cue and everyone in the small private theater. Faith stood up too. We were all standing up clapping at the work Cue had done.

After the clapping was over and everyone regained their composure Cash gave us all a copy of the documentary on a thumb drive. We ate pizza and drank sodas. Cash asked if anyone wanted anything else.

Rome got a call and told everyone he was ready to leave. We headed to the Navigator. As we did Faith touched me on my arm to get my attention.

"You know we're going to be more famous than we are already as soon as Tanza informs her devoted fans that she was a part of this, right," Faith said.

I knew the social media obsessed were now free to tell our unlikely and unbelievable story to the world. Cash and Derricka were already texting and taking photographs. Cue had said, in passing, he was going to send his film to studios.

I nodded. "That was the plan," I admitted.

"You ready for that?"

"Well, I suppose that's the toughest part of being a do gooder," I smiled.

"Yeah, I suppose it is." Faith smiled and chuckled.

Her laugh emboldened me. The sound, the lightness, the joy filled me with certainty. I laughed. I laughed at myself. I laughed at my hesitance after having set a goal, overcome obstacles, made a plan and seen it through.

After all that, it took Allen, the daredevil, to push me and make me realize there was something sitting in the back of my brain for so long which had finally opened my eyes to things I had hoped were real. I stepped forward and grabbed Faith's hand. She looked up. I smiled. I took a deep breath and leaned forward and closed my eyes and prayed I wasn't making a mistake.

www.ingramcontent.com/pod-product-compliance
Lightning Source LLC
Chambersburg PA
CBHW070534100726
47907CB00004B/1117